# THE BUCKBOARD STRANGER

# THE BUCKBOARD STRANGER

## STEPHEN W. MEADER

### ILLUSTRATED BY PAUL CALLE

SOUTHERN SKIES

ISBN 978-1-931177-58-0 cloth
ISBN 978-1-931177- 59-7 paperback

Library of Congress Catalog Card Number 34-8574

Dedication


*The republication of this book is dedicated with love to Alta Atchley Freppon---the greatest sister on earth---by her brother who adores her, Jerry Atchley.*

# FOREWORD

WHEN I WAS a youngster, one of the things I enjoyed
most was to hear my father and mother tell what the
world was like in their childhood. It was better than a
storybook to listen to their tales of trudging miles
through the woods to a one-room country school; en-
countering bears on their berry-picking expeditions; or
being snowbound for days in a lonely farmhouse in the
New England hills.

Later, when my own boys and girls came along, I
found they had a similar interest in hearing about my
youthful escapades. They wondered how a boy managed
to exist and have fun before the days when automobiles,
movies, radio and television became common.

This book is about that period. It is, in many ways, a
faithful account of one summer that was especially
memorable. And while I have given fictitious names to
the characters, some of them will still be recognized by

boys and girls who grew up with me in the little New Hampshire town where I went to school.

That was a background rich in experiences. Some of them have been described in earlier books—"Red Horse Hill," "Lumberjack," and "The Will to Win." Our winters were rugged and adventure-filled, but there were summer thrills, as well. That particular summer, when I had my first rifle and saw my first motion picture, was one of the most exciting.

There really was a "buckboard stranger." He and his Negro retainer, his ten-gallon hat and his horses, appeared out of nowhere, stayed in our midst long enough to win most of the money in town, and left as suddenly as he had come. Whether he really was a desperado hiding from the law we never knew.

To that extent I have embroidered the tale, but in most respects it is a true and accurate picture of the place and period.

*Stephen W. Meader*

# THE BUCKBOARD STRANGER

CHAPTER

# 1

THAT SUMMER was one that Chuck Randall will never forget—not even if he lives to be a hundred. Sometimes it happens that way. A boy grows up in a little, sleepy town where it seems as if the biggest excitement that's ever likely to come along is a brush fire or a strawberry festival at the church. And then, all of a sudden, the days and nights are crowded with action, and one thrill comes after another.

Chuck's right name was Charles Henry Randall and he was about as normal a youngster as you'd find anywhere. He was fourteen in that spring of 1906. Height, around five feet six, and weight, after a big Sunday dinner, in the neighborhood of a hundred and twenty pounds. He had sandy brown hair that was hard to comb, gray-blue eyes and a sprinkling of freckles across his nose.

His family—which was just his father, his mother and himself—lived in half a double house on Second Street

*3*

in the town of Quimby, New Hampshire. The town had been there for two hundred years but its life was so quiet that it never made the headlines. No main roads passed through it and it was sort of off by itself in a rolling country of farms and woods. Two industries supported the population of about a thousand Yankees and French Canadians. One was the woolen mill that stood beside the Narrituck River and got its power from the dam. The other was a series of brickyards along the clay banks downstream.

Chuck's closest friend was an Irish lad named Barney Burke. They had gone through grade school together and both their fathers worked at the mill. Chuck's dad was head bookkeeper and Barney's had charge of the teamsters.

It was early in April that things began to happen in Quimby. New Hampshire winters are long and hard. Snow time gives way to mud time and it seems as if real spring would never come. That year was a little different. Two weeks after the ice went out of the river there were two or three warm days in succession. The wind blew balmily from the south, the snowdrops and crocuses began blooming in dooryards, and Chuck heard a song sparrow one morning. That was on Friday.

"Another week like this," he told Barney on the way

home from school, "and we can start playing ball. You got your glove oiled up?"

"Not yet," Barney chuckled. "There's still frost in the ground. Tell you what, though. I bet the suckers are runnin' in Hanson's Brook. I found my spear in the woodshed an' it's in good shape. Want to go tonight?"

"Gosh—that's a swell idea! Wonder why I hadn't thought of it. I'll dig up my old spear an' bring a lantern. What time do you want to start?"

"Say seven o'clock. Come by my place an' give a whistle."

Chuck went in the back door and through the kitchen, dropping his books on the table. The woodbox was nearly empty and he went out to get an armful of wood for the stove before he did anything else. As he dumped it with a crash in the big red box, his mother's voice called from the front room.

"Charlie, is that you? I thought I'd make brown-betty for dessert tonight. Want to bring me up half a dozen apples from the cellar?"

"Right, Mom," he replied and went down into the half darkness. They had no electricity and it was too much trouble to light an oil lamp. He thought he could find his fish spear without it.

As he groped his way across to the lumber pile in the corner he heard a scurrying noise on the other side of the cellar. It sounded like a rat. He clapped his hands loudly and there was silence.

After a few moments of searching he found the spear. It was a three-pronged affair, hammered out by the local blacksmith, and fitted with a hickory shaft he had made himself. The trident was rough with rust but he knew he could clean it with emery paper and oil. Tucking it under his arm he went over to the apple barrel.

In the fall it had been full to the brim with big, juicy Baldwins and Winter Russets. Now the apples were only a foot or so from the bottom. When he bent over the rim and reached down inside, his hand touched something wet. He snatched it out quickly. Peering in with a lighted match he saw two half-gnawed apples on the top of the pile. And in the side of the barrel, nearly a foot from the floor, was a hole a good four inches in diameter. He studied some of the chips on the floor. They were big chips that looked as if they had been hacked out with a cold chisel, but they had teeth marks on them.

"Wow!" Chuck told himself. "What a brute! No regular rat-trap's going to hold that one."

Hanging on the cellar wall above the work-bench was a No. 2 jump trap that he had used once trying to catch a woodchuck. He rubbed the pan with one of the partly-eaten apples to kill his scent, set the trap and laid it inside the barrel just below the hole. There was a foot-long clog on the end of the chain. If Mr. Rat stepped into that one he was due for a surprise.

Chuck picked out six big, sound apples, took his sucker spear and went back upstairs.

"What's that thing?" his mother inquired.

"Just a spear," he told her hastily. "It's rusty. I thought I'd clean it up."

"Hm-m," she said. "Suckers must be running, I guess. Don't plan to go tonight, do you?"

"Well—yeah, Barney thought we ought to. Why?"

"What about homework?"

"Shucks," he replied. "I've still got more'n an hour before supper, an' anyhow, tomorrow's Saturday."

"All right, do that first. You can get the rust off your spear later."

Chuck knew better than to argue with his mother. She was a kind and gentle woman but she could be very firm when she wanted.

"All right," he said. "There isn't much, anyhow. Just five or six problems an' ten pages o' history."

By the time his father came home from the mill at six, the boy had completed his homework, at least to his own satisfaction. He hurried through supper, rubbed the rust off the old trident and filled a lantern from the kerosene can in the shed.

"I'll try not to be late," he called from the back door.

"But don't wait up for me." Then he ran across the back lot before they had a chance to comment on his parting words.

Actually Chuck was allowed a good deal of freedom. His father, too, had been a small-town boy and knew what boys liked to do. If a youngster got into serious mischief, the punishment was harsh and certain. But if he did his allotted chores, kept up with his school work and appeared on time for meals, his spare time was his own.

There was still a little daylight when Barney came out in answer to Chuck's whistle. They cut around through the fields behind the village so as not to attract too much attention.

"Don't want a pack of other kids trailin' along," said Barney. "All I hope is nobody else has thought o' spearin' fish."

Hanson's Brook was a sluggish stream that meandered through a tangle of alder brush. They reached it at a place where it ran under a plank bridge, on the road west of town. Chuck leaned over the wooden rail and looked down into the water.

"Too dark to see any fish from here," he said. "I reckon we'll have to wade anyhow."

Down under the bridge they took off their shoes and socks and laid them on the bank. Barney felt bottom with his spear. The water was about a foot and a half deep, and swirls of mud followed his probing.

Chuck lighted the lantern. "Br-r-r!" he muttered as he thrust a bare foot in the water. "I don't know as spring's here after all."

In contrast to the balmy evening air the brook was cold as ice. Before he had been in the water thirty seconds his legs were numb to the knee, and he could barely feel the mud oozing around his toes. Shivering, he held the lantern high above his head and stared into the stream.

"Hey!" Barney whispered excitedly. "Over there—isn't that a fish?" And without waiting for an answer he plunged in just below Chuck. There was a splash as he thrust with his spear.

"Shucks—I went an' missed!" he growled in disgust. "I forgot you have to aim lower'n the thing you want to hit when it's under water. What do you call it—refraction or somethin'?"

Chuck made no comment, for he was busy. He had seen a long gray shape nosing slowly up toward the surface, attracted by the light. His trident shot down and he felt it strike flesh. Then the handle was nearly jerked out of his hand as the fish struggled.

"Got him!" he cried triumphantly. "Here—take the lantern while I land him!"

He stumbled up the bank and hauled out a two-pound

sucker. It was a coarse, flabby fish of the carp family. A pair of long feelers or barbels hung down from its mouth like a walrus mustache, and the mouth itself was a sort of nozzle, obviously meant for sucking rather than biting.

Barney came ashore, groaning with the cold. "There's fish in there all right," he said. "You got a pretty good one. Don't call it a 'him,' though. It's a she-fish, comin' upstream to spawn."

They took turns wading up and down the brook and at the end of half an hour they had four good-sized suckers. By that time Chuck's teeth were chattering.

"Satisfied?" he asked. "It's fun spearing 'em but I'd rather quit now than get pneumonia. Suckers aren't worth it. They don't make very good eating, an' I don't know's my ma'll cook 'em."

"I've had enough, too," Barney agreed.

They sat down on the bank and began pulling socks and shoes on their wet, cold feet. The moon was coming up through the alders and off in the swamp to the south the spring peepers made a shrill chorus in the stillness.

"Come on," Chuck urged. "My feet are still numb— let's get walking."

The other boy chuckled. "Don't want to leave the fish behind, do you? I'll cut us a couple o' switches to string 'em on."

He took out his jackknife and trimmed two alder shoots, leaving a hooked fork on the end of each. They were threading the long ends of their sticks through the suckers' gills when a creak of wagon wheels and a muffled thud of hoofs came to their ears.

"Two horses," said Barney. "Somebody comin' up the road with a team. Want to ask 'em for a ride?"

"Not me," Chuck whispered. "Let's lie low an' see who it is."

He had blown out the lantern when they stopped fishing. Now the moon gave enough light to outline every timber of the bridge, a few yards away. In a moment a horse appeared—a tall, raw-boned, dun-colored nag pulling a queer-looking rig. It had no wagon box. Just a couple of long, limber boards sprung to the axles of the four wheels, and a seat mounted a little forward of the middle. A big man sat slouched forward on the seat, holding the reins slack in one hand. He had on a huge, roll-brimmed, high-crowned hat of white felt, and a bandanna was knotted around his neck.

The horse clopped on across the bridge and they saw another figure perched on the tail of the vehicle. The moonlight gleamed on the black skin of a little Negro. He was facing backward and holding the halter of a led horse—a small, slim-legged, short-coupled horse with dust on its dark hide.

The two boys crouched in the bushes and watched, goggle-eyed, as the cavalcade moved off and the sound of hoofbeats faded.

"Ever see anything like that before?" Barney asked.

"Yeah." Chuck hesitated. "In a magazine picture. The rig's the kind they use out West—a buckboard, I think they call it. An' the big feller on the seat was sure dressed up like one o' those Wild West cowboys!"

"But what are they doin' in New Hampshire?" Barney replied skeptically. "Some sort of a travelin' show, you reckon?"

Chuck shook his head. "Search me," he said. "You ready to go home? Let's get started."

They picked up the spears, the lantern and the fish, and set off along the road. Now that night had fallen they saw no need of going around by the fields. Straight into the village they walked, proud of their catch though there were few on the street to see it.

The Neale House was Quimby's one hotel. It was a three-story frame building on Main Street, close to the village square. As the boys passed the hotel stable they saw Mort Kane, the old hostler, holding a lantern in the yard. And its rays fell on the tail of the buckboard, inside the open stable door.

"What do you know 'bout that?" Barney murmured. "Looks like they're stoppin' off here. Wish I could get a better look at that rig, by daylight. An' that colored man—I never saw but one before. He was workin' with a carnival."

"Maybe they'll stay a spell," Chuck told him. "Anyhow, if you get up early enough tomorrow morning, I reckon they'll still be here."

It was only a little after nine when Chuck got home. He lighted the lantern and cleaned his two fish before going in. Then he wrapped them in brown paper and deposited them in the old wooden icebox. He was about to blow out the light when he remembered the trap he had set in the cellar.

Halfway down the stairs he heard a frantic gnawing and scratching in the apple barrel. By the light of the lantern he hunted around for a short, stout stick to use as a club. Then he looked over the rim of the barrel. The animal that glared up at him was at least a foot long and had a broad, flat tail. A muskrat! He hit it hard on the head—one quick, merciful blow—and lifted it out by the clog on the chain. The coat was silky and fine. He knew where he could get half a dollar for such a pelt.

Before he went to bed he skinned the rat and pulled the hide inside out over a shingle that would serve as a stretcher while it dried. Then he reset the trap and went up to his room. He was still wondering how a muskrat had gotten into the cellar when he went to sleep.

CHAPTER

## 2

Getting up seemed to be easier on Saturday mornings than on school days. It was especially easy that Saturday, for the air was still warm with spring and the sunshine outside promised a fine day.

Chuck was downstairs by seven and well into his chores by eight. The woodpile was his responsibility. Along about Thanksgiving time each year the horse-drawn sleds brought several cords of oak and maple and birch down from the woods. The four-foot logs were stacked in a long row beside the shed at the rear of the house. From that time on it was Chuck's job to saw and split the wood to stove size. Part of every Saturday was devoted to this task, and it was usually summer before he had all the wood "fitted" and piled in the shed.

This particular morning he got an early start. He laid a chunk of oak ten inches thick across the battered sawhorse and attacked it with the bucksaw. Three times he

*15*

sawed through it, till it lay in one-foot lengths. When he had a big enough heap of these he laid aside the saw and picked up the ax, splitting each chunk into several pieces.

A quarter of a cord was more than enough to last through the week, but he usually split a few logs extra. It was a good thing to have plenty of dry firewood inside, in case a rainy spell came.

"Charlie," his mother called, as he carried in the last armful. "When you're done I want some things at the store. Here's the list."

He wiped his damp forehead and took the paper. "Any money to pay for the stuff?" he asked.

"You'll have to stop at the mill and get ten dollars from your father. Hurry, now—I need some of the things to start dinner. I suppose you want me to cook those fish I found in the icebox?"

"Sure," he told her with a grin. "They don't amount to much, but the way you fix 'em they'll taste fine."

The short way to the mill office was across the foot-bridge and through the big weave-room. Their house was only a hundred feet from the millpond, and the near end of the bridge was almost in their backyard. As Chuck crossed on the narrow footway, the roar of water plunging over the dam beneath him drowned out the clack of the looms. He stopped to stare down at the frothing white turmoil forty feet below. Then, turning, he chanced to look upstream. The placid surface of the pond was broken by a V-shaped pattern of ripples. He saw a small dark head moving swiftly toward the bank, and as he watched, the animal disappeared in the opening of a drain-pipe, right at the water's edge.

Chuck slapped his fist into his open hand. "That's it!" he exclaimed aloud. "That's our cellar drain. No wonder I'm trapping muskrats!"

He went on into the mill. There was a pleasant smell of clean wool in the air and motes of wool lint danced in the sunlight that came through the narrow old windows. The whole building rocked to the steady thunder of the rows of looms. Men and women weavers nodded to him as he passed, but they never relaxed their vigilance over the flying shuttles. When one of them stopped a loom to tie up a broken end of yarn, the belt screeched on the pulley like a thing in pain.

After the big metal door of the weave-room closed behind him he came into an area of quiet. This was the finishing room, where the huge bolts of flannel and broadcloth were unrolled inch by inch and inspected for flaws, pulled threads or bits of burr. Then they passed through a steam bath and a series of heated rollers that gave them a satiny smoothness—the famous Quimby finish.

Beyond, he went through the shipping room, where

the paper-wrapped bolts of woolen cloth were nailed into great wooden cases, ready to be hauled off to the freight station and sent on their way to Boston.

Finally he reached the office. It was a peaceful, well-ordered room, paneled in dark oak and filled with the musty smell of ledgers. They stood in stately leather-bound rows —a hundred years of business history. Two women worked at typewriters behind the massive oak rail. One of them was Chuck's Aunt Hetty, a spry little gray-haired lady who winked at him as she looked up from her machine. Back of them was a tall, old-fashioned bookkeeper's desk where his father sat perched on a high stool.

The door of the inner office—Mr. Sawyer's office—stood open, and Chuck could see the broad mahogany table and the leather-upholstered chairs. The mill owner wasn't there. He was probably away on one of his many trips to Boston or New York.

His father got down from his stool. "Let him in, Hetty," he said. "I know what he's after."

"Hi, Aunt Het," Chuck smiled, as she opened the gate in the railing. "How's business?"

"Going smooth, as usual," she replied. "Guess you'll be playing ball soon, won't you, with weather like this?"

"Ground's still too wet," he said. "It ought to dry out fast, though, if the sun keeps shining."

His father had gone over to the big iron safe. It was

painted black and the words "SAWYER, QUIMBY MANU-
FACTURING CO.," in old-fashioned scroll lettering, gleamed
on the middle of the door. Mr. Randall turned the dial
backward and forward and opened the safe. He took two
five-dollar bills out of a special drawer and handed the
money to Chuck.

"Take good care o' that, now," he told the boy. "I'll see
you at noontime."

Chuck went out the front door and up the wagon
road toward the town square. He could see the mansard
roof of the Neale House through the lacework of bud-
ding trees. That reminded him of last night and the big
man in the cowboy hat, riding the buckboard. Probably
miles away by now, he thought. One greasy breakfast at
the hotel would be enough for most travelers.

He went into Morse's grocery and butcher shop and
found it busy, as usual on Saturday morning. Two stout
Frenchwomen were chattering in the familiar Canadian
dialect. He recognized one of them as the keeper of the
boarding house at the brickyard. She was buying a fifty-
pound sack of dried peas, a huge slab of salt pork and
enough cornmeal to feed an army. Chuck grinned, re-
membering the rude rhyme he had learned his first day
in school. When a small Yankee wanted to get a rise out
of a Canuck classmate he would repeat it in singsong—

"Pea soup an' johnnycake make the Frenchman's belly ache!"

He was still waiting, list in hand, when he heard a cheerful whistle outside and Barney Burke came into the store.

"Hey," he said as he greeted Chuck, "you know that outfit we saw last night? Well—they're *stayin'* here. Anyhow they might stay a couple o' weeks. I was over at the hotel early to see if they'd left. Mort Kane says the big guy's name's Tex Hawley an' he's from Texas, sure enough. He's just travelin' around, lookin' at the country, an' he thinks Quimby's the kind o' place to rest a while. The little black feller's his servant—sort of a hired man, I guess. His name's Obadiah."

"What did Kane call that rig they were on?" Chuck asked.

"You were right. It's a buckboard, like you said. I got up an' sat on the seat. Sure is a limber contraption— bouncy as all get out, I bet. I got a look at the horses, too. The dun may be a pretty fair roader but he's hammer- headed an' mean. The other's a pretty little mare—sort of a dark chestnut. Mort says she's a saddle horse, never broke to harness. Maybe she's a cow pony, huh?"

Chuck ordered his groceries and paid for them, then waited while Barney did his buying. When they came out

again into the spring sunshine there was a sound of cawing overhead. A great flock of crows went past flying
high.

"Look," said Chuck. "They're headed for the plowed
ground, over by Wilton's woods. I bet we could get a
couple if we went this afternoon. You got anything else
to do?"

Barney grinned. "You know me," he replied. "Any
time there's a chance to go huntin', that's what I want
to do. Bring that pea-shooter o' yours an' we'll start from
my place right after dinner."

Chuck took his bag of groceries into the kitchen and
handed his mother six dollars in change.

"My land!" she exclaimed. "It costs more to feed this
family all the time. With beef at twenty-three cents a
pound, that rib roast I got for tomorrow's dinner came
to more than a dollar! Well, I'll just have to stretch this
money over the rest o' the week."

Chuck tried to cheer her up. "I guess it's a good thing I
brought home those suckers," he laughed. "That's one
meal you don't have to buy, anyway."

He spent the rest of the morning cleaning and oiling
his .22 caliber rifle. It was a bolt-action Savage single shot,
the pride of his heart. He had earned the money to buy it
the summer before by toiling two sixty-hour weeks at a

dollar a day. From the moment he saw it in the hardware store window, he had wanted it more than anything else in the world. Now he spent patient hours with the cleaning rod and oiled rags, keeping the bore bright and the stock and barrel gleaming.

He had half a box of .22 long cartridges and he put in a few shorts to use on tin cans if the crow hunt didn't pan out. Then his mother called him to the noon meal.

The fish were better than he expected. Filleted and fried, with lemon squeezed over them, they tasted so good he had a second helping. Even his father seemed to enjoy them. When the pie was finished, Chuck refilled the woodbox, picked up his rifle and set off for Barney's house.

The Irish boy was waiting for him in the front yard. "I see you got that pop-gun all polished up," he remarked disdainfully. "So slick an' shiny it'll probably scare the crows away. Well—good thing I've got ol' Betsy here to take care of 'em."

He patted the scarred stock of his little Stevens—a hand-me-down gift from his uncle. The boys had an intense rivalry over the merits of their guns. In clear daylight Chuck could always outshoot Barney, for there was a peep sight on the Savage. The older rifle, with its open sight, was a surer weapon when dusk began to fall.

They followed the narrow, sandy road for the first half mile, then cut across an old pasture where juniper and jackpine grew thick among the rocks. From the broken-down stonewall at its farther side they could see the furrows of a ten-acre field, plowed the previous fall. The whole stretch of turned earth was dotted with foraging crows.

"What did I tell you?" said Chuck. "There's hundreds of 'em!"

"Yeah," Barney agreed. "But they'll have sentries out. It's a wonder they haven't spotted us already. Let's try sneakin' around through the woods."

They crouched below the level of the wall and worked their way eastward, expecting to hear the sharp *caw—caw—caw* of the alarm at any moment. Luck was with them, however. They reached the shelter of Wilton's woods without being seen, and went on for several minutes, till they were opposite the middle of the field.

"Ssst!" Chuck warned, pointing ahead. In the bare branches of a big oak a hundred yards away he saw the dark, motionless shape of a sentinel crow.

The two boys got down on their stomachs and crawled cautiously toward the edge of the field. They were sure the thick brush screened them from the eyes of the bird in the oak. But just as they reached a spot where the

plowed ground was in view, there came a sudden clamor
from right over their heads. Looking up, they saw a big
black fellow teetering on a maple limb.

"*Ca-a, ca-a!*" screamed the sentry. And as Barney
whipped up his rifle for a shot the crow flapped swiftly
away.

"Shucks," the boy muttered in disgust. "They always

outsmart us! There goes the whole flock. What do we do now?"

"They won't go far," Chuck told him. "If we let 'em see us move off an' then hide an' wait, I bet they'll be back."

He got to his feet and started to walk away with Barney close at his heels. As they went, the comments of the crow guards followed them. The tone of their cawing had changed now. It still held a note of warning, but at the same time it reassured the flock. "The enemy is retreating," it seemed to say. "They were dangerous—had guns —but we've put them to rout. Better not come back yet. We'll keep an eye on them and tell you when the coast is clear."

For the next two hours the young hunters played hide-and-seek with the wily birds. The first time they took cover they were quickly found out. Broad black wings came sailing over the little open space where they were crouching and a raucous call from the crow scout announced that they were discovered.

"Have to go somewhere else," Barney grunted. "They've got us spotted here."

They crawled away through the brush, trying to find a new and better hiding place.

"Crows are always hard to get, this time o' year," Chuck whispered. "They're all grown up an' wise. Just wait till later in the summer, when the young ones start to fly. That's the time to hunt 'em."

"Some folks say it's wrong to shoot crows," said Barney. "I read in a book they were the farmer's friend— killin' a lot of insects an' mice an' such. You believe that?"

"Partly," Chuck nodded. "Only thing is, they rob corn-fields so bad in the spring, when the young shoots are coming up, that most farmers hate 'em. Dad says there used to be a bounty on crows when he was a boy."

"Gee! I s'pose he made a lot o' money killin' 'em, didn't he?"

Chuck grinned. "Not much," he said. "They were just as cagey then as they are now. I guess nobody has to worry about crows getting to be extinct."

They waited a long time after the cawing of the lookouts subsided; then they started creeping stealthily toward the field again. This time they succeeded in reaching the edge of the woods. The nearest crows were some seventy-five or eighty yards away and in constant motion, hopping from one furrow to the next.

"You want to try a shot?" Barney whispered.

"Pretty far," Chuck replied. "An' they won't hold still enough to draw a good bead. Go ahead if you like."

Slowly and cautiously Barney raised himself on his elbow and brought the little gun into position. A crow hopped to the top of a ridge of earth and stayed there for a second or two. At the crack of the rifle the bird flapped its wings once or twice and toppled into the furrow.

"Got him!" Barney cried. He raced out across the plowed ground and picked up his prize while the rest of the flock flew off in noisy alarm.

"Nice shooting!" said Chuck with a touch of envy.

"They won't be back for quite a spell after that. You want to wait?"

"Sure. Maybe you can get one, too. Anyhow, it's a nice day an' we might as well be here as any place."

A single crow, flying high, came over and cawed the news that he had seen them. Barney laughed. "That spoils this place," he said. "Let's go back in the woods until they settle down."

They found a snug spot in the middle of a clump of bushy young pines and sat on the ground to wait. The sun was getting low in the west now. Soon they would have to start home for supper.

"They don't seem to be making any racket," Chuck whispered hopefully. "Maybe they've come back to the field." He picked up his rifle and started to crawl out of the pine thicket, then drew back. A sudden cawing came from the south, near the lower end of the woods.

"Listen," said Chuck. "I hear wagon wheels. Somebody's coming up the old wood-road."

The narrow, rutted track ran a scant fifty yards from their hiding place. As they lay silently, peering out from under the pines, they heard the creak of wheels draw nearer. Then they could see movement through the brush. A horse came into view. It was a big dun horse, hitched to a buckboard, and the stranger from Texas was slouching on the seat. A few hundred feet away he pulled the horse to a stop and stood up. For perhaps half a minute he watched the road behind him. Then he jumped down, took a shovel and a heavy, square bundle from the buckboard, and stepped quietly into the woods.

# 3

WHAT'S HE UP TO?" Barney whispered. "I can't see him, can you?"

"Just barely. He's over by that big pine. Once in a while I can get a glimpse of his hat when he moves. Reckon he must be digging a hole."

The sentinel crows commanded a better view from the trees where they perched. Their first loud alarm had settled down to a series of less excited calls spaced out at intervals of four or five seconds. They were keeping the flock informed about the movements of this new enemy.

At least ten minutes passed before Hawley returned to the buckboard. Again he paused, looking carefully about him. Then he took the horse's bridle, backed the vehicle around in the narrow trail, picked up the lines and climbed aboard. He was in more of a hurry now. He lashed the big dun with the ends of the reins and went out of the woods at a gallop.

The boys were no longer interested in crows. When the stranger was gone they left their hiding place and hurried toward the spot where he had stopped.

"I guess you noticed," said Chuck, "that he brought back the shovel but not that other thing he had."

"Sure. Must have buried it, whatever it was. Let's see if we can find the place."

They picked up the tracks of sharp cowboy boot heels in the soft ground beyond the wood-road. For twenty yards the trail was easy to follow. Then they lost it on a rocky ledge.

"He couldn't have gone very far," Chuck said. "Circle around an' look for the place he was digging. It ought to show up pretty plain."

But though they hunted for another half hour there was no sign of fresh-turned earth. The sun had set before they gave up and started for home. For a while neither of them had much to say.

"Got any idea what he was doin'?" Barney asked at last.

"Probably nothing to get excited about. But it sure looks funny—a stranger from way out West coming to Quimby to hide something. Oh, well, maybe it was just some food that had spoiled an' he wanted to get rid of it. I remember we had a ham once that wasn't cured right.

Went bad in the icebox an' boy, did it smell! Mom made me dig a deep hole in the backyard an' bury it."

Barney was skeptical. "Yeah?" he said. "You think he'd drive a mile into the woods, an' stop to make sure he wasn't followed? You think he'd go back off the trail an' cover up the place he dug so nobody could find it? That doesn't sound like spoiled food to me. It sounds like gold—or diamonds—or some kind o' buried treasure!"

Chuck nodded. "Sure," he said. "I know. Only that sort

o' thing just doesn't happen in a quiet place like this. What I mean is, if we ever know the answer it'll turn out to be something just as simple as I said."

They got home just in time for supper. After he had finished eating and helped his mother with the dishes, Chuck took a light down cellar and found another musk-rat in his trap. He wondered if it was the same one he had seen swimming toward the drain that morning. He skinned it and hung the pelt beside the first one. If this kept on he saw himself getting rich.

It turned colder in the night, and when Chuck woke on Sunday morning it was raining. He turned over and slept for another hour before his mother called him to breakfast.

Before eleven the Randall family put on raincoats and rubbers, opened umbrellas and plodded across the bridge to the little Baptist Church. A row of buggies and two-seated carriages stood under the long shed, the horses drowsing or munching wisps of hay. There were no automobiles. The town's one car was owned by Mr. Sawyer and he was away.

Inside the church Chuck looked around hopefully to see if the stranger from Texas was present. But all the faces were familiar. Neither Hawley nor the small colored man had joined the congregation that morning.

The rain had let up a little when they came out after the service, but there was no real sign of clearing. Chuck was disappointed. Usually he and Barney went for a hike on Sunday afternoon.

They had finished dinner and the boy was reading a C. A. Stephens story about a Maine moose hunt in *The Youth's Companion* when his friend knocked at the back door.

"Not much of a day," Barney remarked with a grin. "You got anything special to do?"

Chuck shook his head. "Just reading," he said. "Come on down cellar an' take a look at my muskrat skins."

Barney was duly impressed by the two glossy pelts. "Gee," he said, "you keep catching 'em this way an' you'll be in the money."

Chuck laughed. "Sure. One a day would be fine. But I reckon these were a pair, an' I doubt if there'll be any more."

They were on their way upstairs again when Barney got around to voicing what was on his mind.

"I thought you might like to wander up past the hotel," he said. "Somethin's goin' on up there. I heard a couple o' Frenchmen talkin' after mass. Couldn't tell just what it was about, but they sounded pretty excited."

Chuck needed no more urging. He put on his slicker and they went out into the drizzle. The village was quiet enough that day. Most folks were indoors napping after a heavy dinner. But as the boys neared the hotel they saw two or three men moving in the same direction. The men slipped in through the stable yard and went toward a small hay barn at the rear of the premises.

Chuck and Barney saw them knock at the door. It opened a crack and after a low-voiced conversation the men were admitted. Then it closed again.

"See what I mean?" Barney whispered. "You an' me— we'd never get in. But I aim to find out what they're up to. Come on—there's bound to be some place where we can peek in."

They tiptoed past the barn and around to the back. Inside, through the weathered old boards, they could hear a mumble of voices and an occasional low laugh. Then somebody swore loudly and was told to shut up.

The rear of the barn was half hidden by bushes and a tall growth of last year's weeds. Burrowing through the wet stalks, the boys searched until they found a crack in the siding a few feet from the ground. It was long enough for both of them to get a view of the interior.

"For gosh sakes!" Barney whispered. "Look at the crowd!" Chuck couldn't count the men but there must have been twenty-five or thirty of them gathered in the gloom of the barn. In the center of the group a little fence had been built, and inside it the boy could catch glimpses of two men kneeling. A dim glow from a lantern over-head fell on them. Each one seemed to be handling something alive.

Then a spectator moved, giving the boys a better view of the ring. "Chickens!" breathed Chuck. "What in—"

"Sh!" Barney cautioned him. "It's a cockfight, sure as shootin'!"

Inside the fence the small Negro, Obadiah, was strok-ing a scrawny white rooster. Across from him, the other handler held a reddish bird with glossy green neck feathers.

Then they heard a low-pitched, laughing voice above the murmur of the crowd inside. It was the big man from Texas talking.

"Come on, gentlemen," he coaxed, pushing his hat farther back on his head. "We're goin' to have action here right quick. I got another ten to put on the white—anybody coverin' me?"

A red-faced young brickmaker took a nip from a bottle and swaggered forward. "Me—François Gagnon—" he bragged. "Ten dollair on ze red!"

Hawley chuckled. "Good enough," he said. "Hand yo' money to the Majuh, here. He's holdin' stakes."

The "Major" was Mike Doane, the fat hotelkeeper. He had held a commission in the Quartermaster Corps during the war with Spain and come home with enough cash to buy the respectable old Neale House. Some of the other Spanish War veterans in town said he had made his money supplying tainted meat to the Army.

There were no more bets forthcoming and the handlers in the ring crouched lower, holding their birds beak to beak. Then, at a signal, they tossed them loose. The onlookers crowded closer and the boys outside could catch only an occasional glimpse of the furious action. But they could hear the muttered curses and words of encouragement as the fight went on. After a minute or two the voices grew louder, more exultant.

"The white's down!" someone cried. "Look—through the eye—he's finished!"

"Not yet," Tex Hawley said sharply. "Pick 'em up—handle 'em again! A good cock'll fight with one eye if the spur don't hit the brain."

The young Frenchman must have had a few more swigs from the bottle. In a drunken rage he flung himself at the Texan and one of the lanterns fell with a crash, scattering flames in the loose chaff on the floor.

"Quick!" Chuck gasped. "Let's get out o' here—the barn's goin' to burn for sure!"

They ducked out through the bushes and skinned over a back fence. Skirting a neighboring yard, they came out on the street again a hundred yards from the hotel. Men were running in the rain, leaving the scene as fast as they could. There was smoke coming from behind the inn stable. Then the bell in the church steeple across the way began to ring—not tolling but clanging out a frantic alarm.

In the confusion the boys saw three or four volunteer firemen racing up the street with their two-wheeled hose-cart. They coupled on to the hydrant in front of the hotel and pulled the line in toward the burning barn. Chuck and Barney followed them.

It was too late to save the ramshackle old structure, but thanks to the rain the sparks had no chance to set the stable roof afire. All the motley crew who had attended the cockfight had escaped and scuttled out of sight.

After the walls collapsed and the charred embers lay smoldering in the drizzle one of the firemen picked something up from the weeds outside the door. He looked at it curiously. It was a dead white rooster with blood dripping from its beak. On its legs the boys could see a gleam of steel—the long, razor-sharp scimitars of fighting spurs.

*　　*　　*

It took Chuck an hour or more to fall asleep that night, and when he did his dreams were troubled. The brutal business he and Barney had seen was so foreign to quiet old Quimby that it disturbed him.

Neither of the boys mentioned the affair to their schoolmates that week, but there were rumors going around that there was something queer about the barn fire.

On Wednesday after school, Barney called Chuck aside. "I heard my Dad talking to Mort Kane, the hostler, last night," he said. "Mort wouldn't say much, but he made it pretty clear that Hawley promoted the thing. He's a reg'lar gambler. Likes to play cards with the gang at the hotel—doesn't win all the time either. They say he paid off on the cockfight afterward. Just grinned an' said he reckoned it was as good as over when the fire started."

"I wonder," said Chuck, "if anybody's told Sheriff Morgan about it. Cockfighting's against the law, an' old Morgan's tough on lawbreakers. He'd crack down on Hawley quick if he knew, I bet."

"Who'd tell him?" Barney replied. "Not Joe Paley. Sure, he's our constable, but I've got a hunch I saw him in the barn that afternoon. Everybody who was there wants to hush it up, o' course. So I doubt if Morgan ever finds out."

Chuck wasn't so sure. He remembered the queer look on the face of the fireman when he found the dead rooster.

Another spell of warm weather had come after Sunday's rain, and the ball field back of the schoolhouse had dried out enough to play on. They had no regular school team at Quimby, but the boys chose up sides and played some pretty good baseball. Those were the days when the great French batter, Napoleon Lajoie, was famous in the big leagues and every young Canuck in school wanted to follow in his footsteps. The American and Irish boys had their own heroes in such stars as Christy Matthewson, Frank Chance and Bill Dinneen.

"Those French kids are gettin' mighty cocky," Barney remarked as they neared Chuck's house. "They want to get up their own team an' play us Yankees Saturday.

Think we've got nine fellers good enough to beat 'em?"

"Sure," said Chuck confidently. "There's Wash Otis an' Jim Flaherty, both good hitters. Slim Varney likes to play first base an' Wid Gorton does all right at third. Might be a little weak in the middle o' the field, but with you pitching an' me catching we'd have a battery, anyway. How's that curve o' yours coming?"

"Fair, I guess. My arm feels good, too, an' I can whip over the fast ball. Let's practice tomorrow afternoon, soon as school is out. I'll get the word to the rest o' the guys."

Chuck got the battered catcher's mask out of his closet and dusted it off. He hadn't used it yet this year, but in Saturday's game, with Barney throwing the fast one, he knew he'd need it. His mitt had a good deep hole, well blackened with oil of tar. He had never heard of such things as shinguards or chest protectors.

That was the 18th of April, a date made famous by Paul Revere. Before nightfall it had another meaning for millions of shocked Americans. Chuck's father hurried home from the mill at six, his face sober.

"We just got the word from the telegraph office at the depot," he said. "There's been a big earthquake in California. They say the whole city of San Francisco was wiped out—thousands of people dead!"

CHAPTER

# 4

**B**Y THE NEXT MORNING it was all anybody talked about. The sudden rending of the earth—the homes and public buildings smashed and tumbled into rubble—and then the fire that swept through the stricken city, destroying what was left. Three thousand miles away, in the New Hampshire village, the hearts of the good people were touched, just as they were all across the land. The women of the church got together and organized a cake sale to raise money for the sufferers. Somebody passed the hat in the mill and brought four hundred dollars into the office—most of it small bills and silver.

While the pick-up team Chuck and Barney had gathered was practicing Saturday morning, Jean Dubois, captain of the French nine, came over to talk to them.

"How you lak' if we raise some money for dese eart'-quake?" he said earnestly. "Sell teeckets for de game, huh? We mak' folks pay twen'y-five cent for see us—I bet we get some dough."

Chuck sparked to the idea. "Swell!" he said. "What do you say, gang? I'll go fix up a poster an' put it up at the mill gate so folks can see it as they come out at noon. Jean—you spread the word around the brickyards."

He raced home and lettered a large piece of cardboard. "Baseball Game Today," it read. "French Indians vs. Yankee Giants, back of Schoolhouse at 2 P.M. Admission 25 cents, for benefit of San Francisco Earthquake Sufferers."

Those seemed to be magic words. By two o'clock more than a hundred spectators had gathered on the rough, bare field where the game was to be played. Home plate was a square piece of plank pounded into the dirt, and the bases were flat stones. The foul lines were scratched in the earth with a stick.

They had no trouble finding an umpire. Father O'Reilly was acceptable to both sides. He was not only an ardent baseball fan but his parish was about evenly divided between French Canadians and Irish Americans. He flipped a coin to see who would bat first, and the French team won. Barney went out to the mound and started throwing practice pitches into Chuck's big mitt.

Just as the priest was about to order the first batter

into the box, they heard a clatter of horses' hoofs. All heads turned as Tex Hawley, in full western regalia, rode up on his raw-boned dun. Behind him, on the little brown mare, was Obadiah.

"Reckon the ball game can start now," Hawley bellowed jovially. "Here, catch!" He tossed a silver dollar to the boy who was taking admissions. "Keep the change, son. I've been in San Francisco myself."

He swung down from the big stock saddle and handed the reins to the little Negro, who had also dismounted.

The interruption had ruffled Father O'Reilly. From his position back of the waiting Barney he gave the Texan a hard stare. "All right," he yelled, "play ball!"

Chuck signaled for the fast one and it whistled in true for a called strike. Pete Fleury, the lead-off man, gripped his bat harder and waved it menacingly. The next one was meant to be a curve but it was four feet wide of the plate. Chuck asked for another fast ball and got it, but this time Fleury met it squarely. Out in centerfield Wash Otis turned and raced back, but the ball was over his head. Before he could return it to the infield, the runner brought up at third.

The next batter hit a high foul back of home plate that Chuck succeeded in catching. But the third man in the line-up was Jean Dubois. He belted a fly ball to deep

center and Fleury scored after the catch. Above the raucous cheers of the French partisans a heavy voice boomed out.

"Any sports in the crowd?" Tex Hawley was asking. "I've got ten bucks here says the French Injuns'll win. An' I'll give two-to-one odds."

There was a moment's silence. Then a woman's voice answered briskly, "I'll take it. Here's my five dollars."

Chuck looked around, open-mouthed. He was scandalized to see a little gray-haired figure stepping toward the Texan. It was his Aunt Hetty.

Hawley roared with laughter. "Lady," he said, "you keep it for now. I'll see you after the game."

They got the third out on a slow roller to the mound and came off the field for their turn at bat.

"Look," Chuck said to Barney and a couple of the other boys. "Aunt Het must have really got her dander up. I don't believe she ever made a bet before in her life. Come on—we can't let her down. Slim, you're the lead-off man. Get on base."

Slim tried, but he took a called third strike in an effort to wait the pitcher out. Jim Flaherty hit one right into the shortstop's glove and Wash Otis was out on a long fly to left.

Barney settled down in the second and for the next three innings he allowed only one hit. But the score was still one to nothing at the end of the fourth. Try as they would, the Giants couldn't get a man past second base.

"Come on, you Injuns!" Tex Hawley called as Joe Fleury stepped to the plate. "Give us some more runs an' sew this up!"

Chuck knew Barney was trying, but he hadn't had enough practice. There was steam on the fast ball, but little control. He walked Fleury.

The next batter bunted toward third and both runners were safe when Wid Gorton bobbled the ball for a moment. Jean Dubois had a gleam in his eye as he took his stance and Chuck knew he would be trying for the fences. He motioned frantically to the outfielders to move back, then signaled Barney for the curve.

It came up, big and fat, with nothing on it. Jean swung mightily and met the ball. It took off on a long, high arc that gave the desperate leftfielder, Jim Flaherty, time to race back. He made the catch, then threw hard toward third. Fleury had tagged up and was on his way, but he slipped on a pebble, losing a stride. The ball almost beat him to the bag. It was close but the umpire called him safe.

They had men on second and third now and only one out. Big Louis Gagnon watched two wide ones go by and when Barney grooved the third pitch he took a tremendous swing. There was no question about that one. It went over the low fence behind centerfield and lost itself in the weeds for a base-clearing homer.

The French contingent cheered itself hoarse and embraced Gagnon while Wash Otis hunted disconsolately for the ball. At last he found it and tossed it in to the mound. Chuck was there waiting for it, trying to steady his battery-mate.

"Forget the curve," he told Barney. "Just depend on the fast one an' try to get it over. We'll start hitting pretty quick an' give you some runs."

The next batter cut under a hopping fast ball and

blooped a pop-up over second that hung up for the catch. With two gone, Barney breezed two strikes past the hitter, then fooled him with a slow ball that drifted over the corner. They had the side out at last.

With a four-run margin to work on, the French pitcher tried some fancy stuff and ran into trouble. He walked two men in the sixth, and Chuck brought one of them home with a clean single to right. In the top of the sev· enth the Indians scored another run on an error by the shortstop, but the Giants came back with two of their own in their half of the inning.

Starting the ninth the score stood five to three, and the power in the French batting order was coming up.

"How's your arm?" Chuck asked his battery-mate. "Think you can make it?"

Barney looked grim. "It's getting a little sore," he said, "but it'll hold out, I guess. Come on, let's go."

Chuck could see him wince as he threw the first practice pitch, but the ball came in with a sting. The first man up hit a fly that Flaherty caught in left. Jean Dubois took a ball, a strike, a second ball, then lashed a wicked bounder through short for a single. He was dancing on the baseline off first when Lou Gagnon stepped to the plate.

"Come on, boy—another homer!" Hawley shouted. "Smack it out o' the lot!"

The big French boy grinned and swung on the first

pitch. He hit a screaming line drive a yard inside the rightfield foul line, and Chuck's heart sank. It looked like extra bases. But Slim Varney gave it a try. The lanky youngster leaped high in the air and by some miracle the ball stuck in the webbing of his mitt. In two long strides he touched first base. Dubois, halfway to second, was caught flat-footed by the unassisted double play and the side was out.

It was the Yankee boys' turn to cheer. They came racing in from the field and gathered around Slim Varney, pounding him on the back.

"Who's up?" Wash Otis panted. "Let's show these Canucks how to hit!"

"Flaherty's first," said Chuck. "Then you, Wash. Then Gorton. An' save me a turn at bat, won't you?"

Trailing by two big runs, they went up for a last ditch rally. Jim Flaherty beat out a slow roller to third and was safe on a close decision. Otis waited out a three-two count and finally drew a walk. Wid Gorton hit one hard toward first but was out while the other two runners advanced.

It was Chuck's chance. Even a long fly would bring in a run now, but he wasn't thinking about one run. He was thinking about Aunt Hetty and her five dollars. The first pitch almost took his head off. It was high and close —so close he barely had time to hit the dirt. Shaken up but mad clean through, he gritted his teeth and squared off in the batter's box once more. The pitcher missed again with a wide one. Chuck drew a deep breath and steadied down. He had a hunch this one would be in there.

The boy on the mound was a sturdily built youngster named Marty Lachine. He didn't have much of a curve but there was plenty of power in his arm. He could really fog the fast ball over, and that was what he tried to do now.

Chuck saw it coming hard and low, only a shade above the knees. He swung to meet it and felt the solid crack of the bat all the way to his shoulders. There was no time to watch the flight of the ball. He flung the bat away and tore for first, with a rising wave of sound from the crowd giving speed to his feet. There was no sign of a throw to the first baseman. He touched the flat rock that served as a bag and made his turn. It was only then that he got a view of what was going on. In the outfield Lou Gagnon was still galloping in pursuit of the long-hit ball. Flaherty had already crossed the plate and Wash Otis was halfway in from third.

Chuck knew the game was tied but he kept on running as if his life depended on it. Gagnon got hold of the ball at last and threw wildly toward the plate. Lachine knocked it down and tried for a relay to the catcher. He was too late. Chuck crossed standing up, panting hard but grinning as his teammates rushed to greet him.

"Boy, oh, boy!" Barney kept repeating. "A homer in the ninth with two aboard! Darn lucky you did connect, though. I couldn't have pitched another inning for a hundred dollars!"

The crowd was beginning to straggle away. Tex Hawley, still smiling genially, swung up into the saddle and started to turn the dun horse. He appeared to have forgotten all about his wager, but Aunt Hetty hadn't. She reached up a small, wrinkled hand and took hold of the bridle rein.

"Just a minute," she said. "Seems to me you made a bet and the Yankee boys won."

He frowned as if trying to remember. For a moment Chuck thought the man was going to deny it, but there were too many people watching him.

"That's right," he declared. "Five dollars, wasn't it?"

"It was ten," said the little old lady calmly. "Five dollars was my bet and you offered two to one."

Again the Texan burst into one of his big laughs. "Doggone if you ain't right, Ma'am! Here's a ten-dollar gold piece. Catch!"

He flipped the yellow coin carelessly in her direction and she caught it with expert ease.

"Thanks," she told him drily. "Just in case you're interested, this is going in the collection plate tomorrow for the earthquake sufferers." And she turned on her heel and marched away.

Chuck watched Hawley gather the reins and go up the road at a gallop, followed by his retainer on the little mare.

"I thought you said that guy was a good loser," he remarked to Barney. "Did you see the look he gave her when her back was turned?"

His friend nodded. "He doesn't mind losing when he's with the town sports. I guess it must ha' rubbed him the wrong way to have to pay off to an old lady. She sure is a spunky one, isn't she?"

Miss Hetty Randall's bet was the talk of Quimby for the next twenty-four hours. But the gossips' tongues were silenced when the ten-dollar gold piece appeared in the collection at church on Sunday. Even the minister beamed at the sight of it, and when he greeted Aunt Hetty after the service he made a smiling reference to "robbing the Philistines."

Chuck didn't know just what it meant but he gathered that the old lady's fling at gambling was forgiven.

# 5

THE WEEKS PASSED quickly and soon spring was in full tide in the Narrituck valley. Before the middle of May the apple orchards were loaded with pink and fragrant blooms. The boys started going barefoot, and one warm Saturday they could no longer resist the urge to visit the swimming hole.

It was at a bend in the river a quarter of a mile above the town. Clean, yellow sand made a little beach in the shallows, and just below it shelved off into deep water where an old tree jutted out to form a diving board. There were no roads or houses near. Even the approach through the cow-pasture was well screened by alder brush. For that reason nobody ever thought of wearing a bathing suit.

As Chuck and Barney crossed the pasture they could hear shouts and squeals that told them some of the other boys had gotten there first. They broke into a run, unbuttoning their shirts as they went. By the time they reached the bank they were naked as jaybirds.

"Last one in's a—" Barney yelled. But Chuck didn't hear the rest. With a quick look to make sure there was nobody in the water below he took off in a clean dive. The river was a lot colder than the summery air and he came up gasping and thrashing his arms. When Barney's head appeared, a few feet away, they wrestled and tried to duck each other till the first chill was gone.

Four or five other youngsters joined them in a game of water tag. Then they crawled out in the sun to get warm. From a branch of the tree that overhung the water there dangled a frayed piece of heavy rope which Barney eyed with longing.

"Where's the hook?" he asked. "Anybody see it around?"

"It always gets lost," Chuck replied. "Have to make a new one every spring."

He got his knife from his pants pocket and hunted up a ten-foot alder sapling with a branch close to its foot. In a few minutes he had cut and trimmed a serviceable hook long enough to reach the hanging rope.

"Okay," he announced. "I did the work so I get to take the first swing."

He reached out with the pole and hauled in the rope with the hooked end.

"I dunno," said one of the other boys dubiously. "She looks kind o' frazzled."

Secretly Chuck had to agree. But he spoke up with a show of scorn. "You scared to try it?" he asked. "It's always looked like this—for years."

He gave the knot at the end a strong tug or two and nothing happened. "All right," he said, "let's go."

The bank, here beside the tree, was six or seven feet above the river and went off steeply into deep water. The trick was to get a flying start so that the rope would carry far out and return the clinging boy to the bank on the back-swing. If he didn't make it, the penalty followed automatically. He was stranded over the water and had to drop while the onlookers taunted him.

The gang had been so engrossed with the rope that none of them noticed the boat moving slowly upstream. It was a flat-bottomed skiff, hired in the village. At the oars was the black man, Obadiah, and fishing from the stern was Tex Hawley.

Chuck moved back up the bank, took a firm grip on the rope and sprinted down for the take-off. At the last second Barney saw the boat and yelled, "Hey—look out!" But it was too late for Chuck to check his run. He went sailing out over the dark water and just as he reached the end of the swing he heard an ominous snapping sound overhead. The ancient rope was giving way, strand by strand. As the last one parted Chuck was catapulted out into space.

He missed the skiff by inches but the tremendous splash he made when he hit the water drenched both the men in it and nearly overturned the unsteady craft. The fishing rod flew out of the Texan's hand. He gripped the gunwales, trying to keep his balance, and as soon as he had caught his breath he began to swear.

The boys had heard some fancy cursing from lumberjacks and other tough characters, but never anything to compare with the stream of oaths that came from the big man in the boat. Chuck swam a few yards downstream and retrieved the bamboo rod. As he brought it back to the skiff he tried to apologize, but the purple-faced Texan was far too angry to listen. He made a lunge at the boy with his fist and only Obadiah's quick shift of weight kept them from tipping over.

Chuck swam back to the bank. The other boys gave him a hand up and they all stood there grinning until Hawley ran out of breath.

When there was silence in the boat Barney spoke up. "You got no call to get so mad, Mister," he said. "Anybody round here knows this is the town swimmin' hole. An' when that rope busted it was an accident. We weren't tryin' to spoil your fishin'—an' besides, there hasn't been a fish caught here in ten years."

The cold glare that had been in Hawley's eyes was gone now. He drew a hand across his face and the familiar bland smile appeared. In a moment he began to chuckle, then burst into a loud guffaw.

"All right, boys," he told them. "Reckon I lost **my** temper there for a minute. Y' all know where there's good fishin'?"

"You might get a trout up by the riffles," Barney answered. "That's a mile an' a half upriver. An' there's **a** few black bass in Half Moon Pond, over westward."

"I'm right obliged," smiled the Texan, completely jovial again. "Start rowin', you black rascal!"

When the boat was out of sight the boys had a few more dives, but the fun seemed to have gone out of swimming. They dressed slowly.

"Guess we've got to find another rope some place," said Barney. "I'll see if my dad's got a piece around the mill stable."

He and Chuck started home together. For a while they had little to say. It was Chuck who finally broke the silence.

"I don't like that guy," he said.

"Who—Hawley?"

"Right. He puts on a show of being a good fellow, but underneath he's mean an' cruel. You didn't see his face close up, like I did when I was alongside the boat. He'd've killed me if he'd had a gun or a club. I wouldn't trust him an inch."

They were nearly home when Barney changed the subject. "You know what day tomorrow is?" he asked.

"Sure—Saturday. Why?"

The Irish boy's face was red and his eyes didn't meet Chuck's. "Naw," he said, "I meant somethin' else. It's Flossie Kates' birthday."

"Gosh!" Chuck exclaimed. "You're right. What are we going to do about it?"

Florence Kates was the belle of Quimby School. Like the two boys she was in the eighth grade, though she was several months younger. Her father was an expert weaver from England and had a good job at the mill, and his one pretty daughter was the apple of his eye. She was never allowed to go to the boisterous village parties where kissing games like "On the green carpet" and "Post Office" were played. Perhaps it was for that very reason that she seemed extra desirable. Chuck and Barney had been her secret slaves for a year. Both sent her valentines. Both found their eyes wandering to her brown curls in class. And they shared the misery of this unrequited attachment.

Not that Flossie wasn't friendly. Her smiles were warm and she gave them impartially to all her admirers. She was, in fact, something of a flirt under her demure exterior.

"You got a present for her?" asked Barney, drawing patterns in the dust with his bare toes.

"No, have you?"

The Irish boy shook his head. "I thought maybe," he said, "we could go up to her place—take somethin' to eat —make it a sort of a surprise party."

Chuck sparked to the idea. He wouldn't have had the nerve to go calling on the young lady alone, but with Barney it would be different.

"Sure," he said. "I'll ask Mom to bake some o' those special hickory nut cookies. I know Floss likes 'em 'cause I gave her some at lunch one day. What time should we go?"

"I dunno. Get there about eight o'clock, I guess. You think she'll be home?"

"She's always home," Chuck replied. "You know how her folks watch her. But they can't make any fuss about a social call to give her a birthday surprise."

The next evening in the gathering dusk the two boys met outside Barney's door. They were stiff in their Sunday best—collars, neckties, coats and carefully shined shoes. Chuck carried his cookies in a paper bag, and Barney had a similar bundle.

"What're you taking her?" Chuck asked.

"I spent a quarter o' my own money. Got three big oranges. They're really beauts—look."

"Gee," Chuck murmured, "they're nice, all right. Wish I had something as good."

"Don't worry," the other boy reassured him. "I've eaten those cookies an' boy, they're somethin'!"

The Kates' house was a modest story-and-a-half cottage at the northern edge of town. There were lights in the downstairs windows as they approached.

"There she is," Barney whispered. "I saw her go across to the living room."

They tiptoed up on the side porch and stood there, breathing hard.

"You knock," Chuck mumbled. Inside they heard a clock striking eight, and Barney waited till the last chime rang before he gave a timid tap.

It was Flossie herself who came to the door. She was dressed in lacy pink, and to the eyes of the boys she looked prettier than ever.

"Why—" she exclaimed in obvious surprise—"whatever is this about?"

Chuck's throat felt tight in his stiff collar, but he managed a greeting. "Hi, Floss," he croaked. "Happy birthday!"

Barney's voice, saying the same words, came like an

echo, and both the boys held out their offerings, brown paper bags and all.

"We kind of thought we'd bring you a birthday surprise," Barney stammered.

The flustered girl opened the door wider. "Won't you —er—come in?" she said, and they stepped into the bright and spotless kitchen. There were three straight-backed chairs around the kitchen table. When Flossie suggested that they take them the boys sat down gingerly and put their gifts on the table.

Chuck opened his bag. "Here," he said. "Hick'ry nut cookies. They're for you."

"Oh, thank you so much," she smiled. "Let's all eat one."

They heard Mr. Kates clear his throat loudly in the next room and saw him peering at them owlishly over his spectacles. He had on a purple dressing-gown and slippers and was sitting in a big easy chair reading his month-old copy of the *Manchester Guardian*.

The girl fidgeted uneasily. "It's—real nice of you to come," she said at last. "It's been a nice day today, hasn't it?"

They mumbled some sort of a response and helped themselves to more cookies. At that point they were interrupted by the appearance of Mrs. Kates in the door-

way. She was a fussy little lady with frizzed gray hair and earrings.

"Oh," she said. "I thought it was—"

"It's all right, Mother," Flossie put in quickly. "They just stopped by to wish me a happy birthday. Have one of Chuck's cookies."

But Mrs. Kates shook her head. "Come here a minute, Florence," she said.

They whispered for a full minute in the doorway, while Chuck and Barney looked at each other uncomfortably.

There was something about this party that was disappointing to Chuck. It didn't seem to be the gay, romantic affair he had pictured.

When Mrs. Kates had departed they sat down again. "Well," gulped Barney, "only a couple o' weeks more o' school. Next year we'll all be in high school."

"Yes," said Flossie. "And I'm looking forward to it. Of course, I know a lot of boys and girls that are in high school now."

"How you plan to go—ride your bike?" Barney asked. The high school was three miles from Quimby, in the next township.

"Maybe," the girl replied airily. "Several people have offered me rides."

"Oh," said Barney and let the subject drop.

Chuck twisted on his hard chair. "Maybe," he suggested, "we could play some sort of a game—like authors or parcheesi?"

Flossie giggled nervously and looked up at the clock. "Well," she said, "I could try to find the parcheesi set." But she seemed to be reluctant to get up.

At that moment they heard a loud chugging sound outside and a horn tooted. Then there was a brief silence, broken by brisk footsteps on the porch and a knock at the door. Flossie's eyes were bright and her cheeks flushed as she flew to open it.

The young man who stepped jauntily in was a tall fellow who looked at least seventeen. He had on white flannels—"ice cream pants" as they were generally known —and a natty red-striped blazer. Over his arm he carried a linen "duster" of the type worn by motorists of that day.

"Oh, Affie!" cried the girl with a pretty gesture of her hand to her throat. "How nice of you to come to see little me!"

The big youth grinned at her possessively. "Hi, peaches," he said. "You look good enough to eat. All set to go bye-bye? I've got the automobubble running like a watch."

Then his glance swung coolly toward the boys at the table.

"They're just some young neighbors who dropped in," Flossie explained hastily. "Come in and see Father and Mother, Affie. I'll run upstairs and be ready in a jiffy."

Paying no further attention to Chuck and Barney, the young man followed Flossie into the living room and they heard him greet the older people with easy familiarity.

Barney's face wore a black scowl. "I've had enough," he whispered. "How about you?"

Chuck nodded, sick at heart. They got up and started for the door. Then Barney marched back to the table and picked up the paper bag that still held his oranges. With his other hand he grabbed three or four cookies. Then they went quietly out and shut the door.

In the yard a pale young moon shone down on the little car, gleaming with brasswork, that stood in the driveway.

"Oldsmobile," said Chuck without enthusiasm.

"Yeah?" Barney replied. "Who is this 'Affie' guy, anyway?"

"Pitcher on the high school ball team," Chuck told him. "His dad owns the box factory over at Quimby Junction. Guess he's the one that plans to give Flossie rides. Name's Alfred Robbins—you've heard of him."

"Oh. So that's the great Robbins. Here—have one o' your cookies. We might as well save somethin' out o' the mess."

Chuck accepted and took off his collar, tie and jacket, feeling more comfortable again. They walked moodily down the quiet, elm-darkened street. Neither of them found much to say until they were in front of Barney's door. Before he went in he kicked a pebble viciously across the street.

"Women!" he said with pent-up scorn. "To heck with 'em!"

And Chuck agreed from the bottom of his heart.

# 6

MAY MELTED into June and almost before he knew it Chuck found himself on the platform, shaking hands with the principal and bidding farewell to Quimby School. It was a hot evening and his new blue suit seemed to weigh a ton. Flossie Kates gave the valedictory. Then there was a half-hour speech of good advice from the head of the school board, and at last the graduates and their families were outside in the cooler air.

The Burkes and Randalls started home together. Most of the talk was about the boys' summer jobs. In that thrifty New England community it was taken for granted that any youngster worth his salt would work during vacation. Money for a boy's own clothes and a few extras was supposed to be earned between June and September.

"I had my choice," Chuck was explaining. "Dye house, card room or finishing room. Guess which I took."

"You'd be a sucker if you didn't pick the finishing

room. Gosh, the steam in that dye house gets up to a hundred in hot weather! An' I worked in the card room once. Lint up to your knees an' you have to sweep up three times a day."

Chuck grinned. "Okay," he said. "I took the finishing room job. Ten bucks a week. How much are they paying you at the hotel stable?"

"Only eight," Barney admitted. "But I ought to pick up a few tips from sports that rent livery rigs. Anyhow, I'd work for nothing if I could be around horses."

"Yes," Mrs. Burke put in, "and between the two o' them—the boy and his father—ye'd think from the smell we had horses right in the house with us!"

"When do you start?" Chuck asked.

"Tomorrow—six o'clock," Barney replied. "How about you?"

"Same time. I'll be seeing you evenings, though—and week ends."

They parted at the Burkes' door and the Randalls went on home. Chuck was in bed by nine-thirty. He didn't want to be late for work the first day.

Six o'clock seemed to come mighty early, even though the sun was well up and the bobolinks singing. In the finishing room a dour Scotch foreman named MacPherson took the new boy in hand.

"First of all," he said, "ye'll have to learn to lift an' carry a length o' flannel."

There was a huge pile of rolls of cloth at one end of the room. They were gray and khaki mixes fresh from the looms. Each one contained fifty yards of sixty-inch flannel and weighed in the neighborhood of seventy pounds. The old Scotchman gripped one around the middle, swung it to his shoulder and carried it to the nearest inspection table.

"Ye see the way of it?" he asked. "Try one now."

Chuck was awkward at first, but he managed to get a roll on his shoulder and stagger to another table.

"Don't strain yersel'," MacPherson counseled. "It'll come easy when ye have the knack. An' ye'll develop a fine pair of arms an' shoulders by fall."

There were twenty or more slanting tables where quick-fingered women inspected the cloth foot by foot. When each bolt was finished it had to be re-rolled on a long wooden boom turned by power from the overhead pulleys. Then the boom, with its smoothly rolled flannel, was carried on a two-wheeled dolly to the pressing machines.

Between these two jobs, Chuck thought he was frantically busy, but he soon learned he had other chores. At eleven o'clock the foreman called him over and handed him a big watering can and a broom. He sprinkled every foot of the big floor, then swept it clean. This, he discovered, had to be done twice a day—before noon and again before quitting time at night, so that the place would be spick-and-span for the next morning's work.

The sweeping was a full hour's job and he didn't get home for lunch till ten after twelve. In what seemed no time at all he was trudging back to work across the footbridge. That was a long day and by five o'clock when he had to start sweeping again, every muscle in Chuck's body ached with weariness. He thought, with a wry grin, of the time back in the spring when he had imagined he might earn his summer cash just by trapping muskrats. That plan had fizzled out in a hurry. After four rats had been caught, the business came to a sudden end. A week went by without a sign of fur in the trap, and at his father's insistence he had blocked the end of the drain with a heavy wire screen.

He ate his supper and flung himself down on the couch in the living room. In two minutes he was sleeping like a log. How long he slept he didn't know, but somebody shook his arm and he blinked upward into the grinning face of Barney Burke.

"Bushed, are you?" his friend laughed. "'Bout time you learned what an honest day's work is like."

Chuck yawned and sat up. "I suppose you've been sitting around on feed boxes all day," he growled.

"Not me. I had to clean out all the stalls, curry eight

horses, fork down hay from the loft an' lug pails o' water till my arms were like to drop off. Come on out an' get some fresh air. It'll do you good."

It was a fine, cool evening and they sauntered over to the bridge, leaning on the rail and looking down at the water as they talked.

"See anything of our Texas friend?" Chuck asked.

"Yeah. Obadiah saddled up both horses an' they went for a ride about four o'clock. That little mare is really somethin'. They don't let her go very often but I bet she can move like greased lightnin'. I tried to find out more about her from the colored man but he's a cagey cuss. He just laughs an' says she's too small to be really fast."

"Say," Chuck put in, "did you hear about Clint Sawyer, the mill-owner's son? He's home from college with a car he claims can go a mile a minute. An' that's not all —he's got himself a race horse!"

"I know," said Barney. "That's all they were talkin' about at the stable. Clint must be quite a sport. They say he picked this thoroughbred up in a claiming race in New York."

It wasn't just the stable hands who discussed young Sawyer's return to the village. Chuck's father spoke of it at supper the next night.

"I've always liked old Amos Sawyer," he said. "He's a good employer and a good citizen. But after his wife died, he never could bear to discipline that boy o' his. Too bad, too. Young Clinton's run wild so long now, I reckon he's spoiled past helping. What with his gambling and buying cars and horses he'll spend the family fortune in a hurry, I'm afraid."

Saturday noon, Chuck got his first pay. It was only for the part of the week he had worked, but still, those few dollars felt good in his pocket. He knew he was pretty lucky to be getting ten dollars for a sixty-hour week. There were plenty of people in town who remembered when a dollar was a full day's pay, even for skilled work. They still used the old expression, "another day, another dollar," when they left the mill at night. And here he was—a mere fourteen-year-old—getting something like $1.80 a day!

That Saturday afternoon he and Barney went for a long, lazy swim. Then they lolled on the bank and enjoyed the luxury of taking it easy.

"I hear there's a poker game at the hotel tonight," Barney said. "Clint Sawyer's itching to get rid o' some more dough, I guess. Anyhow, he's in it, along with Hawley an' Mike Doane an' four or five others. Let's go up there after supper. They play in the back room, an' there's a window that opens right next to the stable. We could sit there an' listen to 'em awhile."

Chuck knew his parents would disapprove if he told

them, but the idea of eavesdropping on a den of iniquity was too thrilling to pass up. After supper that night he merely mentioned that he was going out with Barney, and not to wait up for him.

Mort Kane, the regular hostler at the hotel stables, was taking his usual Saturday night off.

"He'll go on a binge," Barney explained, "like he does once a week. That's one reason they hired me—to sort o' look out for things while he's out o' commission. By tomorrow afternoon he'll be back on the job, feelin' seedy but able to navigate."

The boys went through the stable, making sure all the horses had enough clean bedding. Most of them were already asleep, some lying down, others dozing on their feet.

"Everything's okay," said Barney. "Now bring along a box an' we'll make ourselves comfortable."

There was a big lilac bush just behind the hotel, and under it the boys placed their seats. A half dozen feet away was an open, screened window through which a light shone brightly. They sat down and waited. After fifteen or twenty minutes there were sounds of men entering the back room—laughter and heavy footsteps.

"Who's got that bottle o' whiskey?" someone asked in a thick voice. "I can't play smart poker till I've got half a skinful."

There was a clatter of glasses and a glug-glug of pouring liquid. Then came another sound—a clicking noise that Chuck didn't recognize.

"That's poker chips," Barney whispered. "Listen."

"I'll start with fifty," said a youthful voice. "Might as well have plenty to bet with."

"Okay, gimme fifty, too," came Tex Hawley's chuckling bass.

"Twenty-five's all I need for a spell," said Mike Doane. And the others followed his lead.

"Two bit ante an' a dollar limit?" one of the players suggested, and there seemed to be general agreement. Knowing nothing about poker, all this was Greek to Chuck. However it sounded wicked enough, and the mention of money indicated they were really gambling.

They cut for deal and Hawley seemed to have won the cut, for he announced that they'd start the hard way. "Straight draw, an' it takes jacks or better for openers," he said above the sound of riffling cards.

"Not me" . . . "By here," one after another of the players replied, until it came to Clint Sawyer.

"I seem to have them," he laughed. "I told you this was my lucky night. Here's a red to start." And they heard the clink of a chip on the table. Everybody stayed in and drew cards.

"Three here" . . . "I'll hold a kicker—gimme two"

. . . "Five cards" . . . and so it went around the board.

Barney got up cautiously and stood on tiptoe to peek through the screen.

"Sawyer won the hand," he reported when he came back. "Raked in quite a pile o' chips, too."

Chuck yawned. "When does the excitement start?" he asked. "Do they just go on like this for hours?"

"Don't worry," the other boy told him. "If the luck runs one way long enough, you'll hear plenty o' cussin' from the rest of 'em. I'd like to find out how that big ol' cowboy acts when he loses money."

In the course of the next two hours Clint Sawyer kept on winning with such regularity that some of the others began to curse their luck, just as Barney had foretold. The young college man himself was almost insufferably gay. He was betting on nearly every hand, and his remarks as he hauled in the chips were not calculated to make his opponents happy.

Finally there was a really big hand. Mike Doane had dealt and called for five-card stud with deuces and one-eyed jacks wild. Everybody stayed in for several rounds of raises, and it was Doane himself who seemed surest of his hand. He kept bumping the pot with blue chips. One by one the other players dropped out, till only Hawley and Sawyer were left to challenge the hotel-keeper.

"Gosh!" Barney whispered from the window. "There must be a couple o' hundred dollars in the pot!"

Chuck joined him to see for himself. The pile of white, red and blue chips in the middle of the table looked big enough to fill a peck measure.

"All right," said Sawyer to Doane at last, "I don't want to take all your money. I'll see you."

"Me, too," said Tex.

Mike Doane laughed triumphantly and spread his hand. "Look at those!" he said. "Four natural aces!"

Hawley tossed in his hand without rancor. "Makes my king-high full house look sort o' sick," he chuckled. Doane started to reach for the chips, but Clint Sawyer was laying out his cards one by one.

"Jack, ten, nine of diamonds," he said, "and two fat deuces. Looks to me like a straight flush."

Doane was on his feet, red-faced and speechless. He slammed the cards down so hard some flew to the floor. Hawley got up and laid a restraining hand on his shoulder.

"You're right, Mike," he said. "It shouldn't happen to a dog—much less a man with four aces. But you were the hombre that called for all those wild cards, so you can't kick if they turn 'round an' bite you. Now sit down an' let's play poker. The night's young yet. How 'bout a drink to cool you off?"

The boys crept away from the window.

"Well," said Barney, "maybe I got my answer. Hawley lost just as much as Doane on that hand—fifty or sixty bucks at least. An' he took it all right."

Chuck stayed for another hour before sleepiness overtook him. In that time the luck seemed to turn a little. The cards weren't coming to young Sawyer as steadily as before. He dropped out of several hands, lost a fairly big one and began to sound peevish when he spoke.

The Irish boy had to stay on awhile to keep an eye on the stable, but he promised to report what happened when he saw his friend the next day. They said good night and Chuck went home.

It was not till after church and dinner that he saw Barney again. The Irish boy looked a little sleepy.

"I stuck around there too long, last night," he yawned. "They didn't break up till two o'clock, an' plenty happened. Along about midnight Hawley hit a hot streak. He bluffed Clint Sawyer out of a couple o' pretty good pots, but then he began to get nice cards. When Sawyer figured he was bluffin' he got fooled. Ol' Tex really had 'em. Man, they took that college boy for plenty before 'twas over! I saw him peelin' hundred dollar bills off his roll when the chips were cashed in."

"Was he sore?" Chuck asked.

"Not very, I guess. I heard him brag there was plenty

more where that came from, an' he wanted to know when the next game would be."

"I s'pose Hawley wound up in good shape?" Chuck asked thoughtfully.

"Oh, sure. He was prob'ly the big winner."

"I still wonder about that guy," said Chuck. "He's no ordinary gambler—more like a professional, I'd say. An' it looks as if he's got himself a real sucker now. Like Clint Sawyer said, there's plenty more money where that came from."

"Yeah. Unless ol' man Sawyer finds out what's goin' on. I bet he'd run that gang out o' town if he knew. Well, all we can do is wait an' see what happens."

CHAPTER

# 7

BY THE LAST of June Chuck felt like an old hand in the finishing room. He not only handled his regular jobs without too much strain but occasionally had time to learn others. The foreman let him take a hand at inspecting cloth when there was a spare table.

It was exacting work. He had to examine every inch of the flannel for bits of burr or other foreign matter that might have gone through the carding and spinning operations. With a pair of sharp steel pincers he could pick out the tiniest scrap of fiber caught in the wool, and he learned to do it without disturbing the weave itself.

Meanwhile the boy had made friends with workers in other parts of the mill. One of his favorites was the old Frenchman who came on duty at six each night and acted as night watchman. Several times Chuck had been a little slow with his sweeping and had to be let out of the building after the doors were locked. Old Jacques was

79

good-natured about it and neither scolded nor reported him.

In return, Chuck sometimes brought him a slab of his mother's pie or a couple of doughnuts to piece out his lonely midnight lunch.

He was talking to Jacques one evening at the end of June when the old man put a finger alongside his bulbous nose and looked at Chuck with a twinkle in his eye.

"Fourt' o' July she's come pretty queeck," he remarked. "How you lak' to ring de mill bell dat night, huh?"

"Gosh!" said Chuck. "That would be swell. Could I bring my friend along, too? Barney Burke—his dad's the stableman—you know him."

The Frenchman nodded. "You can sleep on de wool bags, an' I wake you up when she's time to ring. Don' say nottin' to de odder boys—I ain' s'pose' to let nobody in."

Chuck could hardly wait to get to Barney's that night. The mill bell was a huge one, usually rung with gentle taps that sounded the hours and warned of work time. But with a real swing on the rope it made a terrific clangor—a sound that could be heard miles away. And midnight of the night before the Fourth was one occasion when its mighty voice was let loose over the countryside.

Barney was still at supper and Chuck waited for him

out on the porch. When the Irish boy came out he beckoned to him to follow and led the way down the street.
When they were out of earshot of any of the houses he
gripped his arm.

"Can you keep a secret?" he asked.

"Sure—what's the excitement?"

"You an' I," Chuck told him, "are going to make more
noise than anybody else this Fourth o' July."

"What you got—a giant cannon cracker?"

"Nope. We're going to ring the mill bell—you an' me!"

Barney's eyes popped wide. "Gee!" he murmured.
"How'd you work it?"

"Old Jacques, the night watchman, is a special friend
o' mine. He's going to let us in after dark. We can sleep
on the wool bags until midnight."

"Swell," said Barney, "just so we get out in time for
the bonfire. I'm makin' the doggonedest bull-fiddle you
ever saw. It'll take both of us to work it. Come on back
in the woodshed an' I'll show you."

A "bull-fiddle," sometimes known as a "devil-horn,"
was one of the favorite instruments of torture invented by
New England boys to shatter the eardrums of their
elders on the night before the Fourth. Usually it was an
ordinary tin can with a piece of string, knotted at the end,
run through a hole in the bottom. When the string was
pulled tight and a little rosin rubbed along it, the can

would give forth a horrid sound between a screech and a groan.

Barney figured he had improved on this design. As he showed Chuck, he had used a big five-pound lard pail, and his string was a length of heavy cod-line.

"What I want you to do," he said, "is to hold the handle o' the pail an' pull on it, so the line'll stay taut. I've got a couple o' good chunks o' rosin that ought to make her really holler."

"Let's try it right now," Chuck suggested. "It's finished, isn't it?"

"Well, okay if we do it real easy. I don't want to scare the folks yet."

They shut the door of the shed and Chuck took a firm hold on the wire handle. Barney wrapped the end of the cord around his left fist for a better grip. With a piece of rosin in his right he began gently stroking the tight line. Nothing happened.

"That's funny," Barney muttered. He rubbed powdered rosin into the cord along most of its length. When he tried again the lump of rosin he held flew out of his hand. But his bare fingers slipped an inch or two along the taut line and both boys jumped at the grunting bellow that came from the can's mouth.

"Don't worry!" Chuck exclaimed. "You've got all the noise anybody wants, if you can figure how to get it out."

The Irish boy tried it again cautiously, using his fingers only, and got the same satisfying result.

"Only trouble is," he said, "two or three rubs an' the skin'll be off my hand. It's raw right now."

Frowning he looked around the shed and his eye fell on a pair of old leather work gloves hanging on a nail. Quickly he slipped one on, rubbed a little rosin on the fingers and gave a light pull on the cord. The deafening roar fairly shook the little building, and the boys hid the contraption in haste. They got outside just as the back door opened.

Big Mike Burke came out on the steps and looked at the sky. "Thought I heard it thunder," he remarked, "but I don't see any sign of a storm."

They held their snickers till he was safely back inside, then drifted off through the dark. Up on the hill near the schoolhouse half a dozen boys were working on the bonfire that would climax the celebration of the night before the Fourth. Crates and boxes, old boards and broken fence rails were being dragged in from far and near. Already the pile was nearly twenty feet high, and it would be twice as big before the final night. Chuck and Barney helped carry a decrepit outhouse that someone had found on an abandoned farm. There was a lot of kidding about it, but everybody agreed it would make a fine pinnacle for the top of the pile. At nine o'clock they went home, for both had to be at work early.

*　　*　　*

There were thunderstorms on the first of July and a steady drizzle fell most of the second. The weather was discouraging enough to farmers trying to get in their hay. But to the youngsters of Quimby it was a major tragedy. There sat their huge pile of wood on the hill, getting wetter by the minute. Fortunately the wind swung into the west late in the afternoon, and the third of the month turned out to be hot and fair. Everybody breathed easier.

Chuck had to tell his parents about going to the mill that night. Mr. Randall, who had done the same thing once or twice in his own youth, gave ready consent.

"Maybe you'll be too sleepy afterward to get into much devilment the rest o' the day," he told the boy with a grin.

After supper Chuck made a couple of ham sandwiches and wrapped them, with a quarter of an apple pie, in a paper bag. He and his chum had agreed they would need some nourishment to hold them till dawn.

Barney showed up about eight-thirty when the dusk was deepening. They waited till it was dark, then crossed the footbridge over the dam and knocked at the mill door. After a while they heard steps coming over the

84

creaky floor. Old Jacques opened the door a crack and asked who was there.

"It's me—Chuck Randall," the boy told him in a low voice.

"Hokay," said the Frenchman. "Come in queeck before somebody see you."

They stole inside where the only light came from the watchman's big electric lantern. It was warm and still and smelled of clean wool. Jacques led the way to the big storage room where great bags of wool were piled halfway to the ceiling. There was a little door at one side, opening into the base of the bell tower.

"You go on an' sleep," the old Frenchman told them. "I mak' my roun's every hour, an' I'll wake you hup at quarter o' twelve."

They made themselves snug on the soft bags and the lantern moved away, leaving them in inky darkness. They laughed and talked for a few minutes, but when they fell silent the sounds of the old building were all around them. Soft creakings in the big hewn timbers, small rustlings in the depths of the wool where mice sometimes made their nests.

"Gee," whispered Barney, "it's sort o' scary, isn't it? I'm sure glad I'm not alone in here."

Chuck felt the same way. He doubted if he could have

slept a wink if he had had no companion. As it was, his eyes kept drooping shut and he yawned.

"Let's get a nap," he murmured. "We can eat our lunch when the old man wakes us up."

Within two minutes both the boys were fast asleep.

They woke with a start to see the beam of the lantern shining in their eyes. Old Jacques was chuckling. "Good t'ing I'm aroun'," he said. "You'd be lyin' here till de sun comes up."

Still stumbling with sleep, they followed him through the door into the tower. Two flights of steep wooden stairs led upward and they climbed them in the watchman's wake. At the top they came out on a wooden platform, some ten feet square. High above them in the top of the tower they could see the great black mouth of the bell. The rope hung down to the platform floor.

Jacques turned a switch that lighted a clock on the wall, and they saw that it was ten minutes before midnight.

"Jus' one t'ing," he warned them. "Don' ring until de clock she say twelve. I got to go now. Happy Fourt' o' July!"

They stood there watching the clock after he had gone downstairs. "Wish we'd brought our grub up here," said Barney. "I'm hungry."

"Too late now," Chuck told him. "That old minute

hand's movin' right along. You know that bell's mighty heavy. I bet it'll take both of us to start it."

They practiced gripping the rope to get the best pull. Chuck, who was an inch taller, put his left hand at the top. Then came Barney's right, Chuck's right and Barney's left.

"Like grabbin' a bat when you choose up sides," Barney commented with a grin. "Five minutes to go. The time sure does crawl."

At a minute before twelve they heard distant whoops and yells, followed by a burst of snapping firecrackers.

"Somebody always beats the gun," Chuck grumbled. "But we'll wait. If we don't they'll never let us do this again."

Barney shivered, watching the clock. "Gettin' close," he said. "Maybe we'd better start pullin' to get her warmed up."

They heaved on the rope and the bell moved a little, sluggishly. As it swung back they pulled again, putting all their weight into it. The third time the big clapper struck with a crashing clangor that was all they could have desired.

Now the bell was swinging rhythmically, lifting them clear off the floor at every stroke. It was hard work hanging on, but the giant booming voice above them put

strength in their arms. It filled the night, deafening their ears, shaking the tower, vibrating against their skin.

For ten minutes they rang. Then, breathless and weak, they let go of the rope, working their numb hands to straighten their fingers. The bell kept on clanging for half a minute, then gradually fell silent.

"Gosh!" Chuck tried to say, but his voice sounded small and far off, as if it were coming from another room.

Dizzily they made their way down the stairs and into the dark storage room. As they groped for the pile of wool bags the old Frenchman reappeared with his light and helped them find their parcels of lunch.

"How you lak' it?" he laughed. "Pretty beeg noise up dere, huh? You done good. Made her ring plenty loud!"

He let them out the side door and they crossed the footbridge once more. But this time the night was no longer dark nor silent. A red glow from the bonfire illuminated the town, and a constant blare of horns and crackle of fireworks came from the hill.

The boys paused long enough to gobble their sandwiches, then set off at a run for Barney's house. From the shed they got the big bull-fiddle. Barney stuck a lump of rosin in his pocket, put on the old glove and they set off for the center of excitement. At every step the devil-horn gave out deep, shuddering roars that made householders pop their heads out of windows to see what was passing.

There was a throng of several hundred boys, men and a few girls around the bonfire. It was just reaching its height, with flames shooting far up into the sky, and the heat was so great that they had to keep well away. Shortly after Chuck and Barney arrived the blaze caught the outhouse that formed the pinnacle of the pile, lifted it clear into the air and sent it toppling, to the cheers of the onlookers.

Most of the boys had come equipped with tin horns or firecrackers. A few had bull-fiddles but none that could approach the fearsome racket made by Barney's. He had the champion noise-maker of them all until Tex Hawley rode into the circle of firelight. Suddenly the Westerner let out a high-pitched rebel yell, pulled two big Colt revolvers from his holsters and began firing them into the air. After that, nothing the boys could offer sounded very loud.

The celebration lasted for at least two hours. Finally the bonfire had subsided into a heap of glowing embers and most of the spectators had yelled themselves hoarse.

"Might as well get some sleep," Chuck told his friend. "There'll be plenty going on all day an' we won't want to miss the fun."

"Did you see the way Hawley handled those six-guns?"

Barney asked, as they started homeward. "Obadiah was tellin' me his boss could hit a dime at twenty yards. That I'd have to see to believe, but I still wouldn't want to get in a shootin' fight with the guy."

Chuck heartily agreed. "How's the poker game at the hotel go these days?" he asked.

"I haven't watched it lately but Mort Kane has. He says they're lettin' Clint Sawyer win a little. Not a lot, or all the time, but enough to keep him interested. Mort figures they're settin' the boy up for some kind of a killin'."

Chuck shivered a little in spite of himself. He knew what Barney meant but the word "killing" made him think of the big, smoking pistols in Tex Hawley's hands.

CHAPTER

# 8

CHUCK HAD SPENT a dollar on firecrackers, and after a late breakfast that morning, he shot off a few, just to get the feel of the Fourth. Later in the day there would be a ball game—a team of young men from Norwood coming over to play the Quimby Cubs. Then would come the traditional parade and speechmaking. And in the evening a band concert was scheduled, followed by a fireworks display.

Before noon Barney and Chuck had shot off all their crackers and salutes, scorched their fingers a couple of times, and been approached by half the boys in town to find out how they had got into the mill to ring the bell. Envy made most of them critical of the performance. However, Chuck's father had assured him they had done a good job. "Bounced me clean out of bed," he complained. "I never heard the old bell make more noise."

The ball game was a disappointment. Most of the

Quimby nine were older men, past their prime and out of practice. They were four runs behind in the sixth, when a short, sharp thundershower interrupted play. After it cleared off, some of the schoolboys were sent in to try to stem the tide.

Barney did a valiant job on the mound and Flaherty, Wid Gorton and Jean Dubois put hits together back to back to score two runs in the ninth. However, the game ended with a Norwood victory and the hometown crowd wandered off disconsolate.

The parade started at five o'clock. Chuck had decorated his bicycle with red, white and blue streamers and was on hand promptly to take his place in the line of march at the head of Main Street. Forty or fifty other boys and girls on bikes soon joined him. There was a squad of Spanish War Veterans, stiff in their tight khaki uniforms, and a large section of younger children carrying flags. At the head of the line was Quimby's pride, the eight-piece Silver Cornet Band.

There was a slight delay while they waited for the Grand Marshal. It was Clint Sawyer this year. He finally appeared on his handsome bay thoroughbred, which needed exercise and was hard to control. It danced sidewise across the shady street while the young rider sat very erect and tried to act dignified in spite of his horse's antics.

Riding as flankers were Tex Hawley and Obadiah. The big man on the dun was dressed in full western costume—Texas boots, chaps, calfhide vest and ten-gallon hat. And his small retainer was rigged out as a jockey, in peaked cap, riding breeches and the brightest red-and-blue blouse the boys had ever seen.

A cheer went up from the crowd of onlookers as the three horsemen wheeled into position. Then, at a signal from the perspiring band leader, the trombones and trumpets blared, the drummer walloped his bass drum, and they broke into *Stars and Stripes Forever* with only one or two sour notes.

Down the street past the Catholic Church, the Baptist Church and the hotel, the procession made its noisy way. Chuck was near enough the head of the line to hear the music plainly, but some of the young marchers at the rear had trouble keeping in time with the band. That made little real difference, for the stragglers had their own music, mostly horns, tin whistles and barking dogs.

The parade ended at the center square, where the town fathers and several state dignitaries were already seated in a wooden pavilion decked out with bunting. Chuck motioned to Barney and they wheeled their bikes to the rear of the crowd, away from the speakers' stand. They had heard Fourth of July orations before, and they wanted to be where they could sneak away unnoticed when the speeches got too boring.

They listened through a couple of band numbers and the opening remarks made by the stately Mr. Amos Sawyer. Then, as another speaker was introduced, they eased their way back into the shade of a big maple tree. Others had already left the scene. Back by the hotel they saw the Grand Marshal and his aids standing beside their horses. From the gestures it looked as if some kind of argument was going on.

"Come on," said Chuck. "Let's see what they're up to."

Hawley was talking when they got near enough to over-hear the conversation. "You take any good Kentucky-bred hoss," he said, "an' he's fast over the long distance. Three quarters of a mile—mile—mile an' a half—sure, he'll do all right. But he can't get started fast enough for a short sprint."

"How far are you talking about?" Sawyer responded with some heat. "A hundred yards, maybe?"

"No, no," the Texan laughed. "Down our way we race a quarter of a mile. That's a fair test o' speed."

"And it's your opinion that my Planter's Punch couldn't hold his own in a quarter mile race?"

"He might beat Jughead, here, but he'd never stand a chance with the little mare. She's bred an' bo'n to be a quarter-hoss. Up no'th here, y'all don't understand what that means."

Young Sawyer's face was red. "We know something about good race horses," he replied. "And I never heard of any nag from Texas winning even a six-furlong race."

Hawley shrugged. "Reckon there's only one way to prove who's right," he said, and turned away as if the discussion bored him.

The mill-owner's son rose to the bait. "You want a match race?" he asked. "I'll give you one. My horse is out of condition right now, but let me get him back in training and I'll beat you over a measured quarter of a mile!"

"I s'pose you'll be willin' to back that with cash?" Tex asked softly. "If so, you can set any time you like, an' I'll cover your bet."

"Good!" Sawyer snapped. "We'll say a month from now—the first week in August. We'll measure off a good level stretch of road. Of course I'd be giving away some weight and I'd expect Obadiah to put lead in his saddle. I'll be satisfied if he weighs in at a hundred and fifty."

Hawley smiled. "You don't have to worry 'bout weight," he said. "I'll be ridin' little Mockin'bird myself."

The younger man stared open-mouthed. Then, as his eyes took in the Texan's two-hundred pound bulk, he began to grin. "In that case," he said confidently, "I'll wager a cool thousand dollars, even money. Want to take it?"

"Sure 'nough," Hawley replied lightly. "You got yo'self a bet."

Chuck drew a long breath and turned to Barney. "Looks like some excitement's coming in August." He grinned.

"Golly, yes! I wouldn't miss it for a lot. A thousan' dollars! Gee!"

"Hawley must have an awful good mare or he'd never bet that much," said Chuck. "You think she's got a chance, with that big, heavy guy on her back?"

"Doesn't seem reasonable. But then, as you say, Hawley isn't one to throw cash around careless. Looks to me as if he'd baited Clint into somethin'—maybe a trap. There's lots o' tricks to racin'."

They heard others talking about the bet at the band concert that night. Very few thought Clint could lose, if he had his thoroughbred in racing trim. However, there were some who figured as Barney did. The man from Texas must have an ace up his sleeve, they said.

The band concert was really for an older group of young people—the unmarried men and girls who liked to dress up and walk together to music in the tree-shadowed square. Chuck and Barney and the rest of the boys their age spent the time snickering at the romantic promenaders and sucking lemons ostentatiously in front of the long-suffering tuba player. What they were really waiting for was the fireworks.

It was a hot night, clear and starlit. At nine o'clock when it was dark enough, the crowd moved out to a vacant lot in the upper end of the village. A dozen experts were already there with a wagonload of equipment.

The show started tamely enough with Roman candles and small rockets. Then came bigger rockets, fired four or five at a time, star-shells and cannon rockets that went off with a *boom* at the top of their flight. Pinwheels and "serpents" came next. The grand finale was supposed to represent the battle of San Juan Hill. The uniformed war veterans marched and countermarched, fired a volley or two and then staged a not very convincing charge on the enemy positions. At the same moment the fireworks went off with a tremendous flare of lights and banging of gunpowder. At least it made a grand racket and the boys went home satisfied.

*　　*　　*

With the Fourth over, the summer settled down to the regular routine. Chuck worked his eleven hours every day, had an occasional swim on hot nights, and looked forward to the Saturday afternoons and Sundays that he spent with Barney.

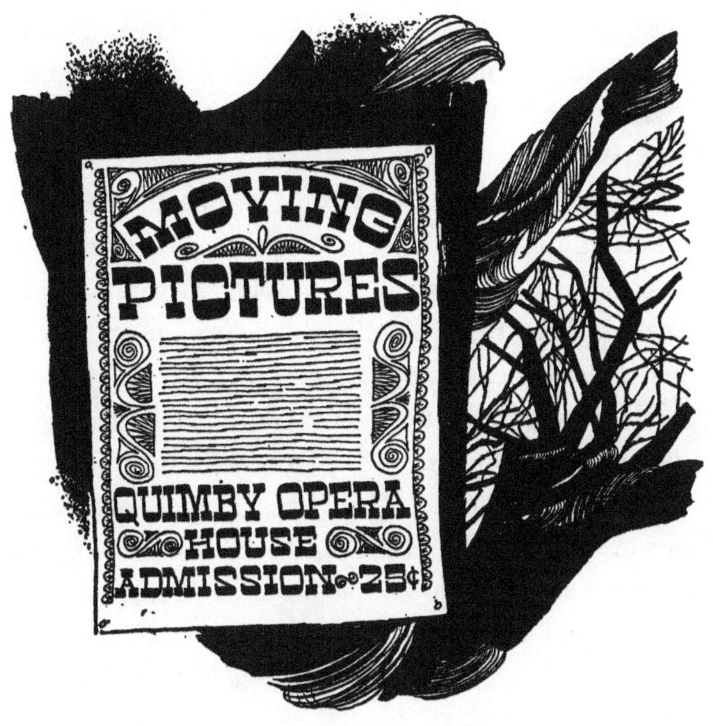


One week end they were on their way to the swimming hole when they saw a man tacking a poster on a
tree trunk. It was a garish thing, printed in red and
black and it announced the showing of an astounding
new invention—Moving Pictures!

"As lifelike as if you were witnessing the actual happening!" read the poster. "Two stupendous subjects: The
Fire Engine and The Great Train Robbery. See the pic-

tures move! Come one—come all! Quimby Opera House, Saturday night. First show at 7 P.M. Admission, 25 cents."

"What is it?" Barney asked. "Just another magic lantern show, I guess."

"No," Chuck assured him, "this is different. My dad read about it in the paper. They've got pictures that really move, just like they were alive. What they use in the camera is long strips of celluloid, rolled up on a reel. There's a crank on the camera that unrolls it an' pulls it past the lens pretty fast. An' every time the shutter clicks —five or six times a second, I reckon—it makes a new picture on the celluloid. Then when it's developed they can run the same roll with a light behind it an' it shows up on the screen with one picture after another, so fast your eye thinks the things in the picture are moving. S'pose they photograph a man walking. You see his right foot on the ground an' his left in the air. Then in the next picture his left foot is going down an' he's up on his right toe, an' so on."

"Hmph!" Barney sniffed. "I bet it wouldn't fool me. You think it's worth two bits to see it?"

"Doggone right. I wouldn't miss this for anything."

Barney was still dubious, but he accompanied Chuck to the show on Saturday night. The "opera house" was a bare room, forty feet square, above a grain and feed store. It had been there for many years, and most enter-

tainments which weren't considered suitable for one of
the churches were held there. The entrance was a flight
of rickety stairs. Folding wooden chairs would seat as
many as a hundred people if they were jammed tightly
together.

There was a barker on the sidewalk outside. "Step right
up, folks, an' get your tickets," he chanted. "The movin'
pitchers are just about to start. Half an hour of thrills
you'll never forget! The most stupendous invention o' the
twentieth century! See the brave firemen an' their horses
gallop down the street to a fire! See masked bandits per-
petrate a train robbery! All for only twenty-five cents—
one small quarter of a dollar!"

The boys bought their tickets and went up the stairs,
where the room was already nearly full. They got chairs
in a rear corner, near a large box-like contraption, covered with black cloth. There was a hole in the front of
it, facing a sheet that had been hung up at the far side of
the room.

"Looks like just another magic lantern to me," grumbled Barney. "I bet it isn't worth a quarter."

"Sh!" Chuck warned him. "Something's starting."

A dark man with a pointed beard and spiked mustache
appeared at the front of the hall and introduced himself as Professor Dufour. He expounded the wonders of
the Moving Pictures in even more flowery language than

the barker outside. Then he took his seat at the old up-
right piano with a flourish of his long coattails.

"While you can see the action on the screen," he said,
"the sounds of these exciting events are lacking. I will
try to reproduce them on the piano as the pictures are
shown. We are now ready to turn out the house lights."

There had been sounds coming from inside the black
box, and now a beam of light shot out, illuminating the
white sheet. At first it was crooked and off to one side,
but after a few adjustments it was squarely centered.
Meanwhile the crowd, largely youngsters, wriggled and
snickered in the darkened room. The professor struck a
few dramatic chords on the tinny old piano. Then, with
a rattle and clatter, the machine went into action. A picture flickered on the screen.

Before their astonished eyes, three white horses came
prancing out of a dark building. Behind them, with
smoke pouring from the brass stack, was a real fire engine. The driver gripped the reins, turning his team to
the right, and two firemen clung to the rear of the engine. While the professor hit the keys in a rhythm like
that of galloping hoofs, the big white team broke into
a run.

At that point the celluloid film broke and it took the
operator three or four minutes to fix it. But there was no

restlessness in the audience. They sat there stunned, murmuring their wonder. The pictures really moved!

There were more views of the fire engine, as it approached the scene of the blaze. Then the horses were pulled to a standstill and the final scene showed the firemen running out their hose.

The Great Train Robbery, which followed, was a more elaborate affair but somehow less satisfying. The actors looked stiff and unreal, and their movements were jerky. Chuck and Barney sat open-mouthed as they watched the train puff to a halt a yard from the log that had been laid across the track. Then two men with bandannas over their faces forced the engineer and fireman out of the cab at gun point.

There was another film breakdown, and when it was mended they saw the bandits tie up the engine crew, move on to the baggage car and finally herd the passengers out on the ballast. Here they were relieved of watches and pocketbooks. In the last scene the two desperados threatened the crew with their pistols, picked up the loot, including a sack marked U. S. Mail, and mounted their horses.

When the lights were turned on again Chuck and Barney sat blinking at each other for a moment. Even the Irish boy was ready to admit now that he had seen something worth all of twenty-five cents. They got up with the rest and filed out, making room for a new batch of customers waiting below.

"What do you think?" asked Chuck. "S'pose they'll ever get this thing fixed up so they can show real plays an' have regular theaters for it?"

"Could be," Barney answered, still in a daze. "If they ever smooth 'em out so they don't jerk so, movin' pictures might be quite a thing. Way it is now, your eyes get tired. I wouldn't want to sit through more'n half an hour. But boy! I'll go back again any time I can see those big fire horses gallop!"

CHAPTER

# 9

THE NOVELTY of pictures that came to life on the screen was still discussed for weeks afterwards by the people of Quimby. But Chuck and Barney found plenty to occupy themselves on their days off without depending on new-fangled entertainment.

Blueberries were ripening in upland pastures, and both boys enjoyed picking them. More than that, when they came home with full pails it meant blueberry muffins and pancakes for breakfast or luscious pies for dessert. Sometimes they took their rifles along on their berrying expeditions. There was no telling when they might see a woodchuck sitting up at the edge of his burrow near a clover patch, or chattering at them from the safety of an old stone wall.

There were gray squirrels in the woods, too, but this was the time of year when the broods of young squirrels were in the nests, so the boys refrained from shooting at the older ones. That could wait for fall, when the leaves were off the trees. They had no such compunctions about crows, however. By the middle of July, the young crows were flying, and offered much better targets than their cautious elders.

One Saturday afternoon they took their twenty-twos and headed toward Wilton's woods. There were young crows there. From nearly half a mile away the boys could hear their raucous squawking. Still they had to approach with caution because the adult birds were very much on guard.

A sentinel crow spotted them crawling through the cover of brush and gave instant alarm. Others, farther away, took up the call, but the young crows continued to caw in cracked, immature voices and it was easy to tell where they were.

Barney pointed to a tall hickory a hundred yards ahead. There was a young crow there balancing awkwardly among the leaves. The boys advanced as quietly as possible, while the warning calls of the older birds grew more excited. At last the black youngster in the hickory left his perch and flapped heavily toward another tree a short distance away. He was obeying orders but seemed to have no idea of the danger that threatened him.

The boys went forward quickly, gaining fifty yards before he had sense enough to move again. Now they were within range, and Barney took a fast shot, stripping off leaves close to the bird's perch.

"Something wrong with that little gun o' yours?" Chuck asked with a grin. "You missed him by a foot."

The young crow teetered on his branch and squawked plaintively but stayed where he was. Chuck drew a careful bead and squeezed the trigger of his Savage. And with a flutter of broad wings, the bird toppled and fell to the ground.

"That's how you shoot crows," Chuck exulted as he ran forward to pick up the victim. "Got him right through the heart!"

It didn't take Barney long to even up the score, and in the course of an hour they each got one more young crow. By that time the quarry was getting harder to find.

"They sure learn fast," Chuck commented. "We've given 'em quite a lesson today, an' I bet if we came back next week they'd be too smart for us."

"Let's cut over to the field, the other side o' the woods, an' see if there's any 'chucks around," Barney suggested.

They worked along the edge of the broken-down wall that bounded the field, but saw no woodchucks near enough for a shot. It was late in the afternoon when Chuck motioned to his friend to be quiet. As they stood there listening a faint sound of hoofbeats came to them through the woods. There was no creak of wheels.

"Somebody on a horse comin' out the old wood-road,"
Barney whispered.

The two boys were hidden from the road by the brush
along the wall, but they could see through the leaves.
After a minute or two they saw Hawley's big dun horse
come out of the woods. The Texan was in the saddle. He
was riding at a walk and looking down at something he
held in his hands. The distance was too great to tell what
it was, but they could see his fingers moving. Then his
hand went to a back pocket where he appeared to place
the object he had been examining. After that he picked
up the reins and urged the horse to a canter, heading back
toward town.

"What do you think he was doing?" Chuck asked.

"Can't say for sure but it looked like he was countin'
money," Barney replied. "Funny thing to do, way back
here in the woods."

"You s'pose he got it from that place where we saw
him hide the box?" Chuck mused. "Maybe that's where
he keeps his cash. There's a poker game at the hotel tonight, isn't there?"

"Yeah. Every Saturday night. Gee, I bet you're right,
at that!"

Barney got a report on that poker game from Mort
Kane the following day. "They're playin' for bigger
stakes," the boy told Chuck. "Some o' the cheaper sports

have been frozen out, an' there's only four or five left who can afford it. Clint Sawyer hit a lucky streak for a while, last night, but Mike Doane an' Hawley won a couple o' big pots later on, an' Clint wound up droppin' a hundred or so. Mort says he just laughed about it. Told 'em not to worry—he'd get it all back when they have that horse race."

Young Sawyer was giving Planter's Punch plenty of exercise those days. Even at six o'clock in the morning, when Chuck went to work, he sometimes saw the handsome bay thoroughbred cantering past with the mill-owner's son in the saddle. Hawley seemed to take the race less seriously. He rarely rode the little mare himself, but let Obadiah work her out on the firm-packed roads north of the village.

"She's fast as lightnin'," Barney told his chum. "Kane says he thinks she could beat Sawyer's horse if she didn't have to carry Hawley's weight."

One Saturday noon toward the end of July, Chuck left the mill with his pay and started across the footbridge toward home. The bigger wagon bridge was only a hundred yards upstream, and he looked in that direction when he heard the plodding sound of many hoofs. Two big, gaily painted wagons, each pulled by four horses, were crossing the bridge. In huge red letters on the side of each wagon were the words, "CHEROKEE SAM'S GREAT

shows." And painted below was the head of an Indian
in the feather war bonnet of a chief.

Chuck sprinted up the path to the main road and overtook the caravan as it started up the hill beyond the
bridge.

"Hey," he called to one of the drivers, "are you going
to be here in Quimby tonight?"

The surly looking man nodded. "Op'ry House, eight
o'clock," he replied and cursed at the tired horses as he
cracked his long whip.

Chuck watched the wagons go on through the village
square. He knew they would make camp at the same
vacant lot where the fireworks display had been held.
When they were out of sight he hurried home to lunch,
and from there headed directly for Barney's.

The Irish boy hadn't heard the news. "What is it?" he
asked. "Some kind of a carnival?"

"I'd say more of a medicine show," Chuck answered.
"Cherokee Sam sounds like a medicine man's name to
me. Anyhow it's not in a tent. It's going to be at the Opera
House. You want to go, don't you?"

"Oh, sure—anything for a little excitement."

They were there early. Admission was only five cents,
so a lot of small fry were in the audience. By seven-thirty
some grownups began to arrive, and activity on the stage
picked up. A fat, dark-complexioned man in western cos-

tume came out and began talking in a loud sing-song voice.

"We're goin' to show you," he intoned, "the genu-wine tribal dances o' the Comanche Injuns. Me, I'm part Cherokee myself, like you'd guess from my name. But Chief Mawgaw, he's a real full-blooded Comanche—used to fight the U. S. Cavalry. Then we'll let you all in on the secret o' health, strength an' eternal youth—Cherokee Sam's own special Injun Rattlesnake Oil. Lemme tell you, if there's anybody here sufferin' from lumbago, rheumatism, sciatica, lame back, swollen joints, fallen arches or any other kind of aches an' pains—one bottle o' this amazin' remedy will make you feel like a yearlin' colt!"

The spiel went on for ten minutes, interspersed with jokes at which Cherokee Sam himself laughed louder than anyone else. When the younger children began to squirm, the showman finally brought a tom-tom out of the wings and announced that Chief Mawgaw would now appear.

The Indian looked impressive enough as he stood erect in the middle of the stage, arms folded, his great feather headdress thrown back. Chuck wasn't sure, but he thought the stern features looked familiar. Was it the wagon driver he had spoken to?

Cherokee Sam began to beat out a rhythm on the

CHEROK
SI

drum and the Comanche bent forward, going into his dance. Gradually he picked up speed, his feet flying to the quickened beat of the tom-tom, the fringes on his leather leggings whipping up and down.

When it was over the Indian stood straight and scowling once more.

"Don't you be scairt, you little folks in the front row," Cherokee Sam chuckled. "He's fierce enough, but I'll see to it he don't scalp any o' you tonight."

The Chief stalked off the stage and the fat man brought out a battered guitar. "I stopped by the hotel this afternoon," he grinned, "an' I see you folks have got a real Texas cowboy 'round here. So I'm goin' to sing you some cowboy songs from the ol' Southwest."

He strummed a chord or two, then broke into *The Old Chisholm Trail*. His voice, surprisingly enough, was a mellow baritone that was pleasant to hear. He followed the first song with *The Cowboy's Lament* and *Home on the Range*.

As he finished, a man wheeled a table in from the wings. It was piled high with bottles of brownish liquid.

"An' now," chanted Sam, "I want to tell you about the world's greatest boon to sufferin' humanity—a powerful panacea for all ills. Yes, sir, it's Cherokee Sam's own special Rattlesnake Oil, scientifically made from those big diamond-back rattlers we have down Texas way."

He went on to describe the wonderful cures brought about by this amazing remedy. There was something almost hypnotic in his rolling words and the shine of his perspiring face under the electric bulbs. At any rate people began to buy Rattlesnake Oil at a dollar a bottle. One of the wagon drivers raced up and down the aisles with armfuls of the stuff, while his boss exhorted the audience with all the fervor of a preacher at a revival meeting.

"My pop gets backaches," Barney whispered. "If I had a buck in my pocket I'd buy some for him."

"Gosh, don't be crazy!" Chuck told him. "This guy's an old fake, an' you know it. The brown stuff in the bottle is prob'ly nothing but kerosene an' turpentine with some kind o' coloring in it."

When Cherokee Sam figured he had sold all the medicine the gathering would buy, he announced the first show was over and the hall must be cleared. "Next show in twenty minutes," he said. "You folks go ahead out an' get some fresh air."

The boys separated when they reached the street. Barney was to get overtime for watching the hotel stable that night. Chuck had something else on his mind. He wanted to check up on that Comanche Indian if he could find him.

There was an alley beside the building, leading back to a rear yard where the medicine show wagons were hitched. It was dark in the alley, and the boy had to feel his way along, resting his hand against the warped old clapboards. He was about halfway through when he heard low voices ahead of him. He recognized the first words as coming from Cherokee Sam.

"Never expected to run into you way up here," the medicine man was saying. "Sure gave me a start."

"Shut up an' listen," a deeper voice replied in a half whisper. "I got a good lay-out here, an' anybody upsets it, he's goin' to wish he'd stayed somewhere else."

Chuck stood frozen against the wall. He knew the second voice. It belonged to Tex Hawley.

"Aw, now," Cherokee Sam murmured, "I ain't plannin' to make no trouble for you, Tex. Just how good is this grift you got?"

"I don't reckon that's any concern o' yours," the bigger man growled. "After your show you're goin' to make tracks out o' here an' forget you ever set eyes on me."

"Okay, okay, but you aim to make it worth my while, don't you, Tex? After all, I've done you more'n one favor. We're old friends, ain't we?"

The Texan swore under his breath and pushed Cherokee Sam back against the wall. "Here's fifty," he muttered. "Now vamoose! An' keep your mouth shut or somethin' mighty unpleasant might happen to you."

The boy was frightened now. He didn't want to get

caught there in the alley. Tex Hawley had sounded deadly serious when he made his threat. As quietly as he could, Chuck made his way back toward the street. His knees were shaking when he finally reached the safety of the crowd outside the Opera House door.

People were going in now for the second show. The boy debated spending another nickel but decided against it, for the hall upstairs was hot and smelly and the show would just be a repetition of the first one. He turned and headed up the street toward the hotel, listening for Hawley's step behind him.

Barney was sitting on a feedbox in the stable door, and he was alone. Mort Kane was taking one of his Saturday nights off. In a whisper, Chuck told the other boy what he had overheard, and Barney's eyes widened at the news.

"Golly," he said, "I bet Hawley *is* hidin' out from the law. If he forked over fifty bucks to keep the medicine man from talkin' he must be really worried. You sure he didn't know you were there?"

"I wish I knew," Chuck answered. "That guy's mean. I'd hate to have him laying for me. But even if he heard me sneaking out o' there I don't believe he knows who it was."

"Think we ought to tell somebody?" Barney asked.

Chuck shook his head. "We haven't got a whole lot to go on," he said. "Most grownups would just laugh at us. I guess the best thing to do is just keep our eyes open an' get some real evidence if we can. I've got a feeling something's going to break pretty soon."

# 10

WHEN CHUCK went to church the following morning he saw that the wagons of the traveling show were gone. Some time in the night Cherokee Sam had hitched up his teams and pulled out.

The town settled back into its drowsy ways and on the surface at least everything appeared to be peaceful. There was a spell of hot weather that week. Horses along Main Street stood half asleep, with heads hung low, and from the trees came the shrill, hot song of cicadas.

Chuck had to use a bandanna often to wipe the sweat out of his eyes as he lugged the heavy rolls of flannel in the finishing room. It was a relief to go out after sunset and cool off in the evening breeze.

The race between Hawley's mare and Clint Sawyer's thoroughbred was still a hot topic of conversation in Quimby. Nearly everybody had begun to take an interest, for the time had been set for five o'clock on the first Sunday afternoon in August. The church people objected violently to the idea of holding it on the Sabbath. A committee called on the town constable in an effort to have the race stopped, but Joe Paley claimed he had no authority to interfere.

"It's just a couple o' gents settlin' a difference of opinion," he told the church folk. "There's nothin' against the law in doin' it on Sunday, far as I can see. Matter o' fact I seem to remember some o' you brushin' your trotters on the way home after service."

That was a telling point. It was true that some of the most law-abiding citizens whipped up their family horses on occasion and tried to prove they were a little faster than the nags their neighbors drove.

Meanwhile the sporting element in the town was getting stirred up over the affair. In addition to the big bet offered by young Sawyer, the boys heard rumors that a number of other men had placed wagers on Planter's Punch. The village barber was one who was ready to gamble a hundred dollars, and there were several more backers for the big bay race horse.

Sawyer continued to train his mount in the early morning, usually on back roads where he could work out in secret. Hawley, on the other hand, seemed to welcome a crowd of onlookers. Each evening before dark he had the mare out on the village streets. He rarely rode her himself, but let Obadiah do the exercising.

A surveyor from the local real estate office had measured off an exact quarter mile on the level stretch of North Street. The start was out on the fringes of town, but the finish line was within fifty yards of the square.

One hot night Chuck and Barney went to watch Mockingbird's work-out. Tex Hawley, smiling and jovial as ever, stood at the starting mark, joking with the crowd of bystanders. It had been agreed that the race would be from a standing start.

Obadiah sat low in the big western saddle, looking half asleep, and the little brown mare stood quiet, though her ears were pricked up expectantly. When Hawley pulled out one of his six-shooters the little Negro gathered the reins and leaned forward. At the crashing report, Mockingbird took off like a scalded cat. Her slim legs flashed so fast they were just a blur in the gray dust, and almost before Chuck could draw a breath she was far down the street.

"Gosh!" he said. "I'm just as glad it's not my money that's being bet. I don't see how anything on four legs can beat her."

"I know," Barney agreed. "Only thing is, she won't be carrying Obadiah in the race. She'll have that big ox aboard an' that'll make a lot o' difference. It's like if you an' I were to race, an' you had to carry one o' those bolts o' cloth you're always gripin' about."

On their way back into town they stopped for a minute in front of the hotel. Clint Sawyer was standing there when Hawley came sauntering down the street. They greeted each other in friendly enough fashion and there was a little good-natured ribbing about their horses.

"By the way," Sawyer remarked, "I suppose you have that thousand ready to pay me."

"I aim to put it in Mike Doane's hands by Saturday night." The Texan's eyes were cold and he was no longer smiling. "I reckon you're satisfied to have Mike hold the stakes? If so, I'd appreciate seein' the color o' *your* cash."

The younger man flushed. "You don't need to worry," he said. "I'll turn it over to Doane ahead of the race. And in case you have any doubts about my ability to raise it, just remember there's usually ten or twelve thousand dollars in the safe, down at the mill."

Hawley turned on one of his genial laughs and slapped young Sawyer on the shoulder. "Okay," he chuckled. "I'm plenty satisfied."

The two boys strolled homeward without much talk. Chuck had an uneasy feeling about the conversation they had just heard. Finally Barney broke the silence.

"That was quite a brag Clint made, wasn't it?" he said.

"Might think to hear him that he owned the mill himself."

"Yeah," Chuck replied. "I doubt if the old man would have liked it—'specially that part about the amount o' cash in the safe."

The first of August came, hot and clear. After a swim one night that week, Barney had a suggestion to make. "If it stays fair," he said, "why don't we camp out Saturday night. I've got that ol' pup tent, an' we could take along bacon an' potatoes an' make pancakes. We could get home Sunday mornin' in time for church."

Chuck heartily agreed with the idea. "Wilton's woods would be a swell place," he said. "I can get Mom to lend me a skillet, an' we'll really cook us a meal. Better bring along a poncho, though, in case there's a thunderstorm."

They made their preparations, and by mid-afternoon on Saturday they were ready to go. The tent, utensils and provisions made a couple of good-sized packs. Chuck guessed his weighed between twenty and thirty pounds. At the last minute they decided to leave their rifles at home and it was just as well, for by the time they had hiked into the woods their packs felt as if they weighed a ton.

"Where do you want to pitch the tent?" Barney asked.

"Any place, just so it's good an' private. How about that snug little place we found last spring, when we were out after crows? Remember? Even the old crow guards couldn't see us in there."

It took them half an hour to find the spot, but when they got there Barney agreed it was worth the trouble. It was a glade, some twenty or thirty feet across, completely shut in by jackpines and young hemlocks. A towering old white pine stood at one side, and its needles, brown and fragrant, made a thick carpet underfoot.

"You go ahead an' pick a place for the tent," Chuck said. "I'll clear the ground here in the middle so we can have a cooking fire. It's been pretty dry an' these pine needles would burn like tinder. Tell you what—I'll make a pile of 'em over here an' we can use 'em for a nice soft bed in the tent."

With great care he scraped away all the needles from an area about six feet square. The bare ground underneath was damp and cool. It would allow them to build a small fire without danger. Next, the boy scouted around in the brush and dragged in a supply of dry firewood. Barney, meanwhile, had set up the little tent on a slight rise of ground and had it well pegged down by the time Chuck had finished his task.

It was nearing six o'clock and the youngsters were getting hungry. They rigged up a fireplace with flat stones, laid out their skillet and other utensils and peeled some potatoes for frying.

"This is goin' to taste mighty fine," Barney said. "Go ahead an' light your fire. Everything'll be ready, time it's good an' hot."

But just as Chuck had the match in his hand, ready to strike, they heard a noise. It was still some distance away but there was no mistaking the creak of wagon wheels.

"Doggone it!" whispered Barney. "I thought we'd picked a real secret place."

"Sh!" Chuck warned. "I bet it's Hawley again. Remember—the wood-road's only fifty yards or so over that way."

They kept quiet, listening to the steady approach of the vehicle. Chuck crawled over to the jackpine screen and found a peephole through the brush. After a moment he beckoned to his friend. Sure enough, it was Hawley's buckboard coming along the narrow track, and the horse called Jughead was pulling it.

To Chuck it seemed as if all this had happened before —as if he knew exactly what would come next. Almost opposite their hiding place the dun horse stopped. Once more, just as he had done months before, the heavy-set man turned and watched the road behind him. Then he climbed down from the buckboard and went into the woods.

Ten minutes must have passed before they saw him again. Barney, growing hungrier by the minute, was restless. "Why don't he hurry up an' get it over with?" he whispered in disgust.

When the big Texan finally reappeared he was walking slowly, holding something in his hand. Before climbing to the buckboard seat he folded the object, whatever it was, and thrust it deep into the pocket of his stockman's pants. Then he went to the horse's head, backed the buckboard around, careful not to scrape against the trees, and walked back to brush over the wheel tracks with his boot. At last he got aboard the vehicle, picked up the reins and drove away.

"All right, let's eat," said Barney with relief.

"Hold on," Chuck replied. "We've still got time to cook supper before dark, an' this may be the best chance we'll have to find out what he's got hidden over there."

"We couldn't locate the place before. What makes you think we can now?"

"Just a hunch. I watched the line he took when he went in. Come on—let's see if we have any better luck this time."

They crossed the woods track and advanced slowly through the trees. Twice Chuck pointed to prints in the earth left by sharp Texas boot heels. When they came to the rocky ledge the tracks disappeared, but Chuck went confidently to the other side. After a minute or two he found another boot print.

"I figure he must have had a marker, so he could find the place easy," Chuck said. "How about that big hemlock up ahead?"

Barney was beginning to catch some of his chum's eagerness. "Sure," he said, hurrying forward, "an' there's some fresh dirt there at the foot of it!"

In a moment they were both digging with their hands in the loose soil. It had been smoothed over as if by a boot sole, and that made them positive they had found the place.

"Feel anything?" asked Chuck.

"I think so. Yes, by golly—something hard an' square!"

They pulled the dirt aside and uncovered a heavy iron box, about a foot long, ten inches wide and six inches deep. The cover was securely fastened by a stout padlock.

"What are we goin' to do with it?" asked Barney.

"Nothing! We're going to put it back just like it was an' cover it up. Tex Hawley'd prob'ly shoot us on sight if he knew we'd found his cash."

He shivered at the thought and stood up to look back cautiously toward the road. The woods were silent and there was nobody in sight. Quickly they deposited the iron box in the hole and rearranged the dirt as nearly as possible the way it had been. Then they made their way back to the glade where their camp was set up.

Soon the fire was blazing merrily and bacon was broil-

ing. Chuck took the stew pan and went in search of drinking water while Barney fried the potatoes. He found a bubbling spring back at the edge of the woods and returned with several quarts of clear, cold water.

They talked in low voices while they ate. The discovery of the box cleared up a number of things they had wondered about. It explained Hawley's previous trips to Wilton's woods.

"He must ha' drawn money out when he lost at poker," Barney said. "An' I guess he put some back when he won. Most likely this time he was gettin' out enough to cover his bets on the race tomorrow. He said he'd have it in Mike Doane's hands tonight—remember?"

"Gosh," Chuck mused. "I wonder how much he's got in there. That looked like bills he took out this time, but I bet there's gold in the box, too. Did you heft it? Must have weighed thirty pounds."

When they finished eating it was almost dark. They stamped out the coals of their fire as a safety measure, then crawled into the tent. The soft, sweet-smelling pine needles under the poncho made a comfortable bed, and somewhere off in the woods a pair of whippoorwills called to each other. Chuck yawned. "I'm ready to go to sleep," he murmured. "How 'bout you?" But Barney was already deep in slumber.

They woke at dawn to the chirping of many birds. The

weather was still warm and the sky clear. Chuck stood up, shook the pine needles off his clothes and stretched luxuriously.

"Boy!" he said. "That was good sleeping. Now I'm hungry again."

"Me too. I'm starved. You go rustle up some more water for the pancakes, an' I'll start the fire."

When Chuck returned he could smell bacon sizzling in the skillet. They had pancake flour, and mixed with water it made fairly good flapjacks. Sprinkled with brown sugar and accompanied by crisp bacon, they were all the boys could ask in the way of breakfast. On his way to the spring, Chuck had spotted a bush blue with big berries.

"Guess we need some fruit to balance these vittles," he told Barney. "I'll go pick blueberries if you'll put out the fire an' clean up the mess."

The morning was still early when they finished eating and took down the tent. They doused the fire and cut back across the fields with their packs. In plenty of time to change their clothes for church they got to Chuck's house.

"See you at the horse race," Barney grinned. "Or don't you plan to be there?"

"Try and keep me away!" said Chuck.

A LITTLE WHILE after noon on that fateful Sunday, there was a short, sharp shower. It cleared off well before race time and its effect was to lay the dust without making the street muddy.

To Chuck's surprise, his father and mother announced that they were going to the affair. Mrs. Randall's purpose was to add her protest to that of the other church women still determined to try to stop the race. Her husband nodded solemn agreement, but he winked at the boy as he did it.

Chuck left the house early and stopped by Barney's but found his friend had already gone. Carriages, wagons and a few autos were coming into town, for word of the sporting event had spread around the countryside. By the time he reached the central square, the space along the curbs was filled with vehicles, and the crowds on the sidewalk were thicker than any seen in Quimby for many years.

As the boy hunted for Barney he saw Affie Robbins' small car parked near the finish line. The tall youth and Flossie Kates, decked out in her best, were giggling and drinking pink lemonade. Chuck finally headed toward the hotel and there was his chum standing near a little group of men. Hawley was among them, and so was Clint Sawyer. Mike Doane appeared to be trying to settle some argument between the two.

The Texan's face was dark. "Nobody mentioned heats to me," he growled. "One dash is the way to run a quarter-hoss race."

" 'Round here," Doane explained, "everybody takes for granted it'll be best two out o' three. That's the way all our trottin' races are handled. Besides, this is such a short distance one o' your hosses might win by a fluke. Two out o' three heats'll really prove which one's better."

For a moment Chuck thought Hawley was going to call the whole thing off. But he looked around at all the hostile faces and changed his mind. "All right," he grumbled finally. "But I've got to have time for the mare to rest between heats. Make it fifteen minutes an' I'll go along with y' all."

The two men were dressed for the race. Sawyer wore trim riding breeches and boots. His opponent had taken off his vest to save weight and had on a gaudy yellow silk shirt, light pants and his great ten-gallon hat.

"Where do you aim to watch?" Chuck asked his friend.

"I'm goin' up to the start," Barney replied. "Come on, let's get good places."

"You go ahead," Chuck told him. "I'd rather watch the finish."

"Heck—look at the mob that's there already. You won't be able to see anything."

"Won't I?" Chuck laughed. "I've got it figured out. See you later."

When Barney had gone, the boy went to a big maple tree a few feet from the finish line. The bark of the trunk was rough enough to afford holds for his hands and sneaker-shod feet. He glanced around to make sure the other boys in the crowd were looking the other way, then quickly climbed to the first crotch of the tree. It was a perfect observation post. There was room to sit in comfort and he could see all the way up North Street to the starting point.

As the time set for the race drew nearer, the crowd under the tree thickened. People were standing on boxes to see over the heads of those in front. From the hotel stables came the horses. Obadiah, strutting proudly in a yellow shirt like the one worn by his boss, led the little brown mare. She looked tiny enough beside the tall bay thoroughbred. Planter's Punch had been curried till his coat shone like satin. At his head marched a wizened little Irishman named Pat Mulligan. For years he had been the Sawyers' coachman, and though he was now their chauffeur, handling the sumptuous Pierce landaulet, Clint had commandeered him as groom for this event.

The bay horse had a little postage-stamp racing saddle that seemed ridiculously small compared to the heavy stock saddle worn by Mockingbird. Behind the horses came their riders afoot. And with them was Joe Paley, the town constable, who would fire the gun for the start.

The little procession had covered most of the distance to the upper end of the street when a disturbance arose right under Chuck's tree. Five women carrying a long white cloth streamer were forcing their way through the crowd. Chuck recognized some of them as members of the Baptist Church congregation.

With fierce determination they pushed the laughing men aside and marched out into the middle of the street, twenty yards from the finish line. There they stretched out their banner and planted themselves solidly across the race course. There were big letters painted on the cloth. They spelled "NO RACING ON SUNDAY."

Cheers and jeers mingled in the shouts of the crowd. Most of the people seemed to take the demonstration as a joke, but there was a grim set to the ladies' faces that made Chuck wonder what might happen.

A quarter mile away, up North Street, the contestants had reached the starting mark and were preparing to mount. The boy could tell them apart easily enough at that distance. He saw Mulligan give young Sawyer a leg up. Then Hawley swung aboard the little mare and they maneuvered their mounts into position.

There seemed to be some delay. Mockingbird was standing quietly enough but the bigger horse danced about nervously and Mulligan had to hold him by the bridle. After perhaps a minute of this Chuck saw the little Irishman jump aside. There was a puff of smoke from Paley's revolver, followed a full second later by the report. The crowd yelled "They're off!" and everybody strained forward to see the start.

The mare with her big rider was coming like a streak. But Planter's Punch had shied at the gun and got away several strides in the rear. They were at the halfway point now and the bay horse seemed to be closing the gap. Tex Hawley leaned far forward in the saddle to cut down wind resistance. He snatched off his hat and batted it against the mare's flank, letting loose a high-pitched rebel yell at the same moment. The sound of it, and the sight of the two horses rushing down upon them, must have unnerved the embattled women with the banner. They broke for the curb like a flock of frightened chickens, leaving their bold message in the street. An instant later it was trampled by flying hoofs, and the heat was over. The two judges, standing on opposite sides of the finish line, walked out to compare notes. Chuck already knew the answer, for he had had a perfect view of the finish. The mare had won by nearly ten feet.

Mike Doane, who was acting as one judge, held up his hand for silence and finally got the crowd quieted. "The first heat," he announced, "goes to Mockingbird by three-quarters of a length!"

Cheers and a hubbub of excited talk followed. Somebody went out into the street and dragged away the tattered remnants of the banner. Chuck felt a little sorry for the ladies who had so valiantly tried to stop the race. He caught a glimpse of one of them now. Her bonnet was askew and she was cheering excitedly with the rest.

The horses were being walked slowly back up North Street by their grooms. Planter's Punch looked less fidgety now, though he was sweating a bit. The mare's coat, too, was darkened by moisture, and an edge of white lather showed beside her loosened saddle girth.

Looking down from his perch, Chuck saw Barney working his way through the crowd, apparently searching for somebody. He leaned down, pushing the leaves

apart, and gave the whistle they used to call each other.

Barney saw him and grinned. "Any more room up there?" he asked. "I guess you had the best idea, after all."

In a moment he was up on the limb beside Chuck. "Gee," he said, "this is a swell spot. I couldn't tell who

won from up the street there. I hear it was Hawley. But what was that white thing the women were holding?"

Chuck described the whole affair, much to his chum's amusement.

"Was your Aunt Hetty in the bunch?" he asked.

"Not her," Chuck laughed. "Aunt Het likes horse-racing almost as much as baseball. Tell you one thing, though. If she had been one of 'em, she'd have stuck it out. Dead or alive, she'd still be hanging on to that banner! What happened at the start o' that first heat? I was afraid Sawyer'd be left at the post."

"It wasn't that bad," Barney told him. "The gun scared his horse a little but he got rollin' pretty quick. Boy, how that mare took off, though—like a singed jackrabbit!"

"Think she can last long enough to win another?"

Barney shook his head. "I wouldn't bet too much on it," he said. "With anything like an even start, the big horse ought to take her."

The fifteen-minute rest period seemed longer to the waiting throng. People down on the sidewalk couldn't see what was happening and kept asking others if the heat had started yet. Meanwhile the two boys in the tree watched the grooms rubbing down their horses and re-adjusting the girths. Hawley and Sawyer were standing well apart, no longer talking to each other.

"Suppose they're sore about something?" Chuck asked.

"Could be. Before the first heat they were like a couple o' strange dogs. Polite, but that's about all. I reckon Hawley's still riled up about havin' to win two out o' three. If he'd had his way it would ha' been all over by now."

Now they could see the riders getting ready to mount. This time the bay horse stood more quietly, though Mulligan still held his bridle. Paley lifted his arm but there was no puff of smoke or sound of a shot. That made no difference to Mockingbird. She was off and running. The boys saw her rider lean back, pulling on the reins, and inside a hundred yards he had her stopped.

"The constable's ol' gun prob'ly misfired," Chuck said with a grin. "That mare's so keen to run she started when the hammer clicked. Boy, will Hawley be sore now!"

From the Texan's gestures, as he rode back to the mark, it looked as if Barney was right. He shook his finger in Paley's face, took the revolver and examined it, then handed it back and maneuvered the mare into position again.

Planter's Punch had reared and pranced a little when the smaller horse took off. Now he appeared steady again. There was another pause of a few seconds, then the gun was fired.

This looked like a much evener start than the first one, and Sawyer's backers in the crowd shouted and waved their arms, urging the bay horse on.

"Here they come!" Barney yelled in excitement. "All even—maybe a dead heat!"

But as they thundered into the final fifty yards, Chuck saw Clint Sawyer cut down on the bay with the whip.

The big thoroughbred responded. It was close, but he stretched his long neck out and crossed the line a yard or so in the lead.

That was how the judges called it, too. "Planter's Punch by a neck," Doane told the crowd. "Heats are even. This third one'll have to decide it."

Both horses were well lathered now. Obadiah walked the little mare back and forth, crooning to her softly, and Mulligan wiped the flecks of foam from the bay horse's chest.

"I'm going to get down an' walk around a little," said Chuck. "My left leg's asleep from this hard branch. Save my place if any kids try to get up here."

He scrambled down and stamped his foot on the sidewalk to restore the circulation. At that moment a babble of excited talk behind him attracted his attention. He looked around and saw the town barber and the railroad freight agent in the center of a huddle of men.

"He had his show here just a week ago last night!" the barber exclaimed. "Doin' all right, but not gettin' rich, far as I could see. Who'd want to rob a medicine show anyhow?"

"What happened?" asked a newcomer, and Chuck crowded in closer to hear the answer.

"Killed," the freight agent answered. "Shot clean through the head. I got it off the telegraph wire a spell ago. Seems a farmer found him, 'bout five o'clock this mornin'. He was haulin' a load o' milk to the creamery an' saw the show wagon pulled off the road an' the team tangled up in the harness, tryin' to browse off the brush. He got down to look the rig over, an' there was this fat man lyin' on the seat with blood under his head an' all over the cushion."

"Cherokee Sam, was it?" the other man asked. "Where'd it happen?"

"He was found on the road about a mile outside o' Norwood. They put on their show there last night. The other wagon an' the rest o' the crew had gone on ahead an' they claimed they didn't know a thing about it. There's just one feller the sheriff hasn't located yet—that Injun Chief What's-his-name. Some think he was the one that did it."

Chuck had heard enough. He ran back to the tree and climbed up as fast as he could. Barney seemed surprised to see him back so soon.

"You look like you'd seen a ghost," he remarked. "Somebody after you?"

"You didn't hear what those men were talking about down there," Chuck said, "or you'd have looked the same way. Listen—Cherokee Sam's dead—murdered!"

Barney's face lost its smile. "Whew!" he whistled softly. "You don't suppose it was—"

Chuck looked scared. "Don't talk too loud," he warned. "He's still down there with the mare. Yeah, he could have done it. Only about ten miles away an' it happened last night or early this morning. They haven't found Chief Mawgaw anywhere around an' I guess the sheriff figures he's the man to catch."

He went on to tell all the details of the murder as he had heard them.

"If the Comanche was ridin' the wagon with Cherokee Sam, maybe he got shot, too," Barney suggested. "I think you ought to tell somebody about what you heard in the alley that night."

"Who?" Chuck asked. "Paley's too dumb to know what to do, an' anyhow he's a pal o' Hawley's. I wish there was some way to get word to the sheriff. Maybe it would have been better if I'd told my dad right at the start."

"Well, there's nothing we can do right this minute," said Barney. "They're takin' the horses back to the start an' everybody'll be watchin' this third heat. I bet that little ol' mare is plenty tired right now, even with the rest she's had."

Chuck looked down at the crowd. All heads were turned toward the upper end of North Street. Even the knot of men who had been discussing the murder had now dispersed to get a better view of the race. There was only one person in sight who didn't seem to have the same interest. He was a tall stranger in a dark coat and a black soft hat. Its broad brim concealed his face, but the boy was sure he was no local resident. He leaned against the corner of a building and watched the excited crowd without moving.

Chuck wondered who he was and what he was waiting for.

## CHAPTER

# 12

**F**OR THE NEXT FEW MINUTES the boy gave no more thought to the stranger in the black hat. Along with all the rest of Quimby's population he was looking up North Street, eyes glued to the starting line. The saddled horses were there now, together with their grooms and riders. The Texan acted as if he were in no hurry to mount. He stood rubbing his hands up and down Mockingbird's legs and patting her sleek neck. Finally, after Clint Sawyer was in the saddle, the constable went over to Hawley and pulled out a watch, apparently reminding him that the quarter hour rest period was more than past.

Even then, the big man took his time. When he finally threw his leg over the cantle and settled himself, there was a sigh from the crowd. This was it—the big moment of the thrill-packed day. They waited for the puff of smoke from the starter's gun, then broke into a chorus

*144*

of cheers and shouts that drowned out the sound of the shot.

It looked like a good start. From their vantage point in the tree, the boys could see better than the people on the ground, and the horses were neck and neck halfway down the course. Then something happened. The big thorough-bred's forefoot must have struck a loose stone, for he stumbled, almost tossing Sawyer over his head. He re-covered quickly and was back in stride a second or two later, but the distance lost was too much to make up in that final furlong. The little mare finished a good length in front.

With the race over, everyone swarmed out into the street, surrounding the horses and their riders and rais-ing such a racket that nobody heard the judges' official announcement. That made little difference, for all those present had witnessed Mockingbird's victory.

Dismounted, Tex Hawley led the mare back to the finish line through a tumult of cheers and backslapping. The only long faces in the crowd belonged to young Saw-yer and the local sports who had bet on him.

After a moment or two the mill-owner's son worked his way to the center of the group, where Hawley was standing with Mike Doane.

"Tough luck, Clint," the Texan chuckled and held out

his hand. "Reckon you'd ha' took me if it hadn't been for that stumble."

Sawyer ignored the offered hand. "Pay him off, Mike," he told the stakeholder coldly.

"What—right here?" Doane asked. "Hadn't we better go over to the hotel? You know—these crazy women—"

"Pay him now," said the young man. "I want to see him pocket his money. It's the last of mine he'll ever get."

The conversation was taking place almost directly under the tree where the boys sat, and they could hear every word in spite of the babble of the crowd. As Mike Doane reached somewhat uncertainly for his wallet, Chuck saw the tall stranger again. He had left his post beside the building and was edging quietly into the group around the contestants.

Doane began to count out large bills. "Eight hundred, nine hundred, a thousand o' yours, Tex," he said. "And here's the other thousand Clint gave me."

He had put the money in Hawley's hand when the man in the black hat moved in.

"Just a minute," he told them in a voice that had the ring of authority. "I'd like to take a look at some of those bills."

"An' who might you be, buttin' in like this?" the big Texan asked truculently.

The newcomer pulled back the lapel of his coat and Chuck saw a flash of bright metal.

"United States Marshal," he replied. "Now the money, please."

The crowd had wedged in closer, open-mouthed with astonishment. Leaning forward from their tree crotch the boys saw Obadiah, still holding the end of the mare's reins, slip in behind the black-hatted man and crouch on all fours.

"Look out!" Chuck tried to yell, but he was too late. Hawley's arm shot out and he gave the marshal a violent push that sent him toppling backward, heels over head.

Then a lot of things happened all at once. The little colored man sprang up like a cat and jumped into the saddle. With a yell he forced the little mare straight through the crowd. People fell over each other trying to get out of the way. And by the time they collected their senses both Obadiah and the Texan had vanished.

The marshal didn't get up. He lay there where his head had struck the curb and a little trickle of blood oozed from under his black hat.

"Quick!" shouted Mike Doane. "Get a doctor—an' fetch some water, somebody."

Fortunately old Dr. Timmins was in the crowd of spectators. He hurried over and knelt beside the prostrate

officer. "Hm, pulse is all right," he announced. "Just knocked out, I guess. Maybe a concussion. Let's look at that head."

A further examination showed no fracture, and when a French brickmaker produced a pint of whiskey, the doctor poured a little into the mouth of the unconscious man. He stirred, opened his eyes and sat up groggily.

"Take it easy, now," Dr. Timmins warned, but the marshal shook his head impatiently.

"I'm okay," he said, "and I've got a job to do. Anybody see where they went?"

Barney had already dropped down out of the tree. "I did!" he said. "They cut through that alley—headed for the hotel."

At that moment Joe Paley arrived on the scene. He had followed the racers down North Street on foot and he was out of breath.

"What's goin' on here?" he puffed. "Who's this man? After all, I'm the constable here."

The man in the black hat was on his feet now.

"Glad you're here, constable," he said with a wry grin. "I'm Dolan, U. S. Marshal. You and I have got a job to do. I wanted to see the numbers on those bills because they may have been stolen from a bank in Kansas City last March. We've been trailing a man that answers this Hawley's description. His real name's Hickson, an' he's got a long crime record. Finally we got word he might be hanging out around here. How long was I knocked out?"

"Not more'n four or five minutes," Doane told him. "But you'd better hurry before they get too much of a start."

"All right. Let's try the hotel, constable. You can come

along, young fellow. But the rest of you keep out of the way. There might be some shooting if they're still there."

Barney, proud to be allowed in their company, ran ahead. He looked around for Chuck but his friend was nowhere in sight. He remembered then that Chuck had jumped down when the excitement first started.

Dolan and Paley were close behind him when he reached the hotel stable yard. The buckboard was gone and so were the dun horse and the little mare. The only human figure in sight was the elderly woman who cooked for the hotel. She stood there in the yard twisting her hands in her apron, a look of fright and horror on her face.

"Did you see Hawley leave here?" the marshal asked her quickly.

"Oh, yes," she replied, half crying. "Him an' the colored man. They were in an awful hurry, seemed like. Hitched up the big horse to the buckboard with their saddlebags on it. An' that poor little feller that tried to stop 'em!" She broke off with a sob.

"What's that?" Dolan asked sharply. "You mean a boy got mixed up in this?"

"He snuck up while they were harnessin' and tried to cut the traces with his knife," she said. "They grabbed him an' tied his hands an' feet an' flung him on the buckboard, too. An' then the feller called Obadiah jumped on the little horse an' away they went."

"Which way?" asked Paley.

"Down that way, past the mill. They haven't been gone more'n a minute."

"Got a car, constable?" Dolan snapped. "Never mind, mine's back here in the square. But before we start I'll call the sheriff to block the roads. Telephone here in the hotel? Good." And he ran up the steps.

Barney went to the cook's side. His voice was trembling as he asked her a question. "The—the kid they took on the buckboard—did you get a look at him? 'Bout my size? Sandy hair?"

"That's right," the woman replied. "I thought it was the Randall boy but I couldn't be sure. Anyhow they didn't—didn't shoot him."

*　　*　　*

Chuck lay face down on the bouncing buckboard. His head ached from the blow that had knocked him down, and the rope on his wrists had chafed sore places. For the moment he was too groggy to know which road they were taking, or care what they meant to do with him. He thought hazily of rolling off the limber planks, but with the dun horse at a gallop there was a good chance

151

the rear wheels would run over him. Also he knew that Obadiah, on the mare, was right behind.

As his mind cleared he thought back, trying to figure how he got into this jam in the first place. When Tex Hawley knocked the marshal down and got away in the confusion, Chuck had been one of the few who saw where he went. He knew they would make a dash for the hotel to get Hawley's horse, and without any real plan he decided in that split second to follow them. He was sure others would be right behind him.

When he got there he realized the pair must have expected to make a quick getaway. The buckboard was standing in the yard, with the saddlebags stowed under the seat. And when Hawley came hurrying out of the stable leading the dun, he saw that the horse was already harnessed. Obadiah got off the mare to help back the big nag into the shafts and hook the traces, and for a moment both men were on the off side where they couldn't see Chuck.

That was when the boy made his mistake. He had a desperate feeling that somehow he must delay them till help arrived. On an impulse he ran forward, crouching, pulled out his pocket knife and hacked away at the heavy leather of the near trace. But before he could cut it a quarter through, the colored man came around the rear of the buckboard.

Chuck tried to duck the blow and failed. It caught him on the side of the head. Dazed but still struggling, he heard Hawley snap out an order. "Quick—tie him up," the Texan had said. "We'll take him with us."

That was the part Chuck couldn't understand. Why had they wasted even the half minute it took to whip a rope around his wrists and ankles? They could have hit him again and knocked him out. Somehow Hawley must have a plan to use him.

They were well out of the village now. The boy turned his head so that he could get a glimpse of the passing fields and knew they were heading for Wilton's woods. That made sense. The Texan would hardly go off and leave that box. Chuck wondered if Barney wouldn't figure the same way and bring the law officers in time to catch them there.

The buckboard turned in on the wood-road and went bouncing over roots and chuck-holes, nearly knocking the breath out of the boy. When it stopped he saw Hawley jump down from the seat and start into the woods.

"I'll be back in a minute," he called to Obadiah. "Keep watch behind there, an' holler if you see anybody comin'."

Hopefully Chuck listened for the shouts of pursuers. But the woods were silent except for the cawing of crows and the rustle of the evening breeze among the leaves.

It didn't take Hawley long to return. He came out of

the brush carrying the heavy iron box in his arms. It still had a layer of dirt on it when he deposited it alongside the saddlebags under the seat.

They didn't turn back toward Quimby this time. Hawley whipped up the dun horse and they rattled on through the woods, scraping against tree trunks and bumping over rocks. The wagon track hadn't been used for years, Chuck thought. He had a momentary hope that the buckboard would get stuck or break down, but it was a toughly built affair. After perhaps ten minutes of this kind of travel, the ride suddenly smoothed. They were out on the stubble of a hayfield.

Hawley put the horse to a gallop once more. He seemed to be in a hurry to get out of this open country and into the sort of cover they had had in the woods. They passed a dilapidated old hay-barn and came out on a stretch of graveled country road. Chuck didn't know just where they were but he figured they must have covered a total of three or four miles since leaving Quimby.

The road seemed to have very few farms along it. They passed nothing but young pine growth and brushy pastureland in the half mile they traveled before turning off into the woods again. This was real forest—big pines and hemlocks with a sprinkling of hardwood. The trees met darkly overhead and the narrow logging track over which the buckboard jounced was gloomy with shadows. Chuck realized suddenly that night was coming on.

Hawley and his dun horse seemed to know where they were going. The pace varied between a trot and a fast walk, depending on the roughness of the ground. But the big nag didn't hesitate or stumble, and the mare, trailing close behind, was equally sure-footed.

Suddenly the Texan pulled up on the reins and they swung to the right, out of the rutted track.

"Here we are," said Hawley. "Get her unsaddled, Obie, an' give me a hand with the rig."

He turned to look down at Chuck and appeared satisfied with the way the ropes were holding. In the half darkness the boy could see some kind of low shack beyond the horse's head. Obadiah was uncinching Mockingbird's saddle. Now he led her quickly forward and into the shack. It must have a dirt floor, for there was no sound of hoofs.

In a moment the two men unhitched Jughead and he followed the mare inside.

"You take care o' the buckboard," Hawley told the colored man. "I'll get the kid in. The grub's in one o' the saddlebags."

Before he laid a hand on Chuck, the Texan took the iron box from under the seat and carried it into the shack.

Then he returned and picked the boy up like a sack of meal.

"You just keep your mouth shut an' lay still," he told Chuck as he dumped him on the floor. "Nothin's goin' to happen to you—not yet, anyhow."

CHAPTER

# 13

HAWLEY TOOK MATCHES from his pocket and lighted a candle. Its glimmering light fell on a wall of small logs —little more than poles, really—chinked with mud and bark. From what Chuck could see of the roof, it was made of more poles, covered by wide strips of bark. And the floor, as he had guessed, was nothing but trampled earth. A sort of partition fenced off the part of the cabin they were in from the stable end, but he could plainly hear the horses champing hay on the other side of it.

There was no furniture except a pair of bunks made of rough lumber at one side of the room, and a battered old sheet-iron stove at the other. The place was, Chuck realized, a choppers' shack, used in winter by the Frenchmen who cut wood to supply the brickyard kilns. How Hawley had found it he had no idea.

Obadiah disappeared for a few minutes and came back with a bucket of water. Then he brought in a paper par-

*157*

cel tied with string and a tin can labeled "Choice Peaches." Hawley opened them both with his knife and helped himself to a thick sandwich out of the paper.

"Here," he told the colored man, "go ahead an' eat. An' you might as well untie the boy's hands so he can manage one o' these, too."

When the rope was off Chuck's wrists he sat up, rubbing the chafed spots, and accepted the sandwich Obadiah offered him. It was a slab of roast beef between two pieces of unbuttered bread, and though it didn't taste very appetizing he ate it all. There was no telling when he would get fed again. The colored man gave him a drink of water, then tied his hands behind him once more.

Meanwhile the big Texan consumed several sandwiches and started on the peaches. He would stab a half peach with the point of his knife and pop it into his mouth, then wash it down with some of the sweet juice, smacking his lips noisily. He didn't offer any of the peaches either to the Negro or to Chuck. When he had finished he tossed the can aside and it rolled close to the boy's feet near the piece of string that had tied the sandwich parcel.

"Well," he said, after a comfortable belch, "here we are, all safe an' snug. Short o' bloodhounds, I reckon it'll be a right smart while before they locate this place. An' by then we won't be 'round."

Obadiah looked scared. "You say bloodhounds, Mist' Tex?" he asked with a shiver. "Ah don' like dem big dawgs, nohow."

Hawley chuckled. "I bet there ain't a bloodhound this side o' Boston," he said. "You can quit worryin', Obie."

"You gwineter do dat job tonight, Mist' Tex?" the little man asked.

"Shut up," Hawley growled. "No. We're goin' to stay right here tonight an' lay low. Another twenty-four hours an' they'll think we're fifty miles away. So I aim to rest the hosses tonight an' tomorrow."

He got up from the bunk on which he had been sitting, hung his big hat on a peg and yawned mightily. Then he strolled over toward Chuck.

"If you're wonderin' why we brought you along, kid," he said, "it's easy. I knew they wouldn't shoot an' chance hitting you if they got too close on our heels. Soon as things cool off a little, we'll let you loose. But until then, just watch your step. Keep quiet an' lay still."

He leaned over, tested the boy's bonds, then yawned again and threw himself into the bunk.

"Blow out that candle, Obie," he said, "an' stay awake. You'll take the first watch. Gimme about four or five hours an' then wake me up. You can sleep after that."

*　*　*

Barney waited outside the hotel. It wasn't long—only a minute or two—before the marshal came out. He must have a tough head, the boy thought, for he looked healthy enough as he bounded down the porch steps and started for the square at a run. Paley had already gone on ahead to find the car.

Barney fell into step beside the tall man. "Wait—Mr. Dolan," he panted, "I think I know where they went!"

Dolan glanced at him but didn't slow down. "You do?" he asked. "Why?"

"Because Chuck—that's the kid they took with 'em—Chuck an' I, we found where Hawley has his money buried. It's down in Wilton's woods. An' I bet that's the first place they'd head for—to pick up that cash."

The marshal nodded. "We'll try it," he said. "I want to hear more about this but you can tell me after we're in the auto. There it is, over by the curb."

The machine was a small touring model—a one-cylinder Cadillac with seats for four people. Dolan instructed Barney to get into the back seat and Paley to sit up forward with him. He set the spark lever and hurried to the left side, where he spun the starting crank several times. The little engine under the seat coughed once or twice, and finally, after a full minute of cranking, it rattled into action. The marshal hoisted himself up to the driver's seat and released the brake.

"Here we go," he said as he put the car in gear. "Now give me the facts about this money you say Hawley—or Hickson—buried."

"Well," Barney explained above the noise of the car as it banged down the street, "Chuck an' I were huntin' crows the day after the buckboard came to town, an' we saw Hawley carry somethin' heavy into the woods an' bury it with a shovel."

"Something heavy," Dolan commented. "How'd you know it was money?"

"We didn't, then. But last night we were campin' out down in the woods, an' before sundown we saw the guy come back to the same place. He didn't know we were there but we could watch him. He came out to the buckboard countin' bills that he folded up an' put in his pocket. Prob'ly it was the thousand he bet on the race. After he'd gone we went over an' found where he'd dug in the ground. We pulled out an iron box with a padlock on it. It was pretty heavy—like it had gold or silver in it. Anyhow, we stuck it back in the hole an' covered it up."

They were nearing the road that led into the woods, and the boy told Dolan where to turn in. The car had to move slowly over the ruts and bumps. A spring wagon rode better, Barney thought, though he was too polite to say so.

"Looks like you were right," the marshal said. "Fresh wheel tracks and hoof-prints. How much farther?"

"Only a little way," Barney told him. "There—that's the place, right ahead."

Dolan left the engine running and jumped down. "They're not here now," he said, "but they can't have gone very far. Let's see about that box."

Barney took him to the foot of the big hemlock and

they found an empty, yawning hole there. The dirt on the edges was still moist and fresh.

"Not more than five minutes old!" the marshal exclaimed. "Now the question is, where did they go from here?"

Joe Paley was studying the ground along the woodroad. "They were here, all right," he announced. "Two sets o' hoss tracks, an' all headed the same way. Guess they must ha' gone right on through the woods."

Dolan frowned. "Don't know whether we can make it with the auto," he said. "Does the road get much rougher? Well, there's only one thing to do, and that's try it."

Back in the car they moved slowly on along the rutted trail. The buckboard tracks showed up plainly, and they could see places where the wheel hubs had scraped bark off the trees. As the going got worse, the engine stalled twice and had to be cranked back to life.

Finally Dolan gave it up. "We're going to get stuck sure if we keep on," he said. "Here's a place where I may be able to turn around, and it's probably the last chance. We'll try to pick up their trail where it comes out of the woods."

He backed the little car into an opening between two trees, went forward, backed again and at last had it headed out the way they had come.

"Do you know where that road leads?" he asked Paley.

"Never been through it myself," the constable replied, "but there's a county road over there about a mile. We'll have to go pretty near back to Quimby to reach it, though."

They got out of the woods without accident and Dolan ran the car at top speed toward the village. Soon they were on a crossroad that took them to the county highway.

"Not many folks live along here," the constable said. "It's barren soil, too poor to farm, mostly."

They passed a field where an old hay-barn stood, but that was the only building they saw for some distance. It was getting toward dusk, now, and the gloomy pine woods on both sides of the road made the evening still darker. At last they came to cleared land and a small farmhouse near the road. Dolan stopped the car and went to the door, which was immediately opened by an old lady.

"Evening, Ma'am," he greeted her. "Did you happen to see anybody pass here in the last few minutes? A buckboard and somebody riding a small horse along with it?"

"No," she replied positively. "I been settin' right here by the window watchin' the road. Gets mighty lonesome here, an' I like to see folks go by. But your autymobile is the first thing I've laid eyes on in 'most an hour."

The marshal frowned. "Ma'am," he said, "I don't mean to doubt your word, but are you sure you haven't left the window at all?"

"Well, now," she answered, "Come to think of it, I did go out to the kitchen a spell ago—just to let the cat out."

"How long ago?"

"Oh, maybe five minutes, but I wasn't gone long an' I didn't hear nothin' go by on the road."

Dolan thanked her and went back to the car. "That pretty well fixes the time they must have passed here," he said. "Let's get going—we may be able to catch up with 'em. Anyhow, they won't get out of the county. The sheriff says he'll have all the roads blocked."

*　　*　　*

Chuck found it hard to get to sleep. Not only was the floor uneven and rough, but with his hands bound behind him he could lie only on his side or on his stomach. His head had stopped aching but he was tired, sore and hungry. And he had plenty of worries to occupy his mind.

As far as his own safety was concerned, he thought Hawley might have been telling him the truth. In that case all he had to do was endure his present misery a little while longer and he'd be free. However, there were others to consider. His mother, for instance. She must be frantic by now. His father would probably take the news more calmly, but he'd be pretty upset inside. And there was Barney—what would he be doing? Nothing rash enough to get him in trouble, Chuck hoped.

He went over and over the happenings of the last twenty-four hours, and was surer than ever that Hawley had murdered Cherokee Sam. Not only that—if a U. S. Marshal was after him, he must have committed other crimes. Chuck shivered and thanked his stars the big Texan hadn't seen him that night in the alley. He doubted if he would be alive now.

The light was out but he could hear Obadiah stirring restlessly from time to time, yawning and mumbling under his breath. From the bunk came the rumble of Hawley's steady snoring.

Chuck must have fallen asleep at last. But his slumber wasn't too sound, for he woke an hour or two later when he heard low voices. He lay there listening, trying to breathe loud and evenly so that they would think him still asleep.

"But, Mist' Tex," the colored man was whispering, "ah hates to see yo' go back dar tomorrer night. Why ain' we better off lightin' out right quick?"

"Obie, you ol' fool," Hawley answered, "the last place they expect to see me is back in Quimby. By tomorrow they'll be huntin' for us in Vermont an' Massachusetts. Besides, the money's sittin' there, waitin' to be taken.

One ol' watchman is all they got. With that much cash, an' what we've got now, we'll be well fixed for life. Soon as the job's done we'll take off for Canada. There's plenty o' places to get across the line. Now you go to sleep an' I'll stand guard."

Chuck heard the bunk creak as he lifted himself out of it. Then there was the flicker of a lighted match. Hawley tiptoed across to look at the prisoner, seemed satisfied that the boy was asleep, and went away again.

After what he had caught of their conversation, Chuck's brain was more than ever in a whirl. Back to Quimby tomorrow night. That could mean only one thing. Hawley meant to rob the safe at the mill. The boy remembered with a sick feeling how young Sawyer had boasted about the amount of cash kept there. Then he thought of poor old Jacques, the watchman, who had been so good to Barney and himself. What would happen to him if he tried to stop the robbery?

It was all the boy could do to lie there motionless and pretend he was sleeping. But his weary body gave in after a while and he really slept.

The next time he woke was in the gray of a cloudy dawn. He heard Obadiah talking.

"Boss," he was saying, "ah don' like dis yere shack— it's got ha'nts! All night long ah kep' hearin' 'em. Dey was moanin' an screamin' fit to skeer me to death!"

"Stop it, you idiot!" Hawley commanded. "All you had was a bad dream. I was wide awake the whole time, an' there wasn't a sound, outside o' maybe a hoot-owl or two. Now get out o' that bunk an' rustle some breakfast. No fire, though. We can't afford to have any-body see smoke in here."

Still grumbling about "ha'nts" under his breath, Obadiah got up and produced more sandwiches from the saddlebag. Again Chuck's hands were untied, and this time the colored man freed his ankles as well. The sand-wiches were getting dry by now, but at least they were nourishing. With plenty of water to wash the food down, Chuck began to feel better.

"You go outside an' wash," Obadiah told him. "Ah'll be right wid you to see you don' run off."

Chuck's legs felt so numb from their long confinement that he had difficulty walking. When he returned to the shack the ropes were put back on him and he lay down once more. Hawley had gone to his bunk to catch up on his sleep, and Obadiah was in the stable end of the cabin looking after the horses. An idea had come to Chuck while he was eating breakfast. Cautiously he stretched out his feet and pulled the empty peach can over to him. The piece of string lay a little farther away, and by roll-ing over he was able to reach it. Then he returned to his original position and acted as if he were taking a nap.

Actually his hands, hidden behind him, were constantly busy. The rope that tied his wrists was half-inch manila but well worn and a little frayed. He didn't want to cut it yet. What he was doing was practicing—training his fingers to use the sharp edge of the can lid, so that when evening came he could free himself.

CHAPTER

# 14

THE MARSHAL'S little Cadillac had a top speed of only about twenty-five miles an hour. On rough country roads and in sand or mud it was considerably slower, though to Barney, used to horse-drawn travel, it seemed as if they were going like the wind.

It was close to eight o'clock and beginning to get dark when they pulled into the town of Norwood. During the five-mile drive Barney had had a chance to tell Dolan about Chuck's experience in the alley by the opera house, the night the medicine show was in Quimby.

"Why didn't he tell me about it?" Paley demanded from the front seat. "It might ha' saved Cherokee Sam's life."

Barney squirmed. "We talked about tellin' you," he said, "but we both figured any grownup would just laugh at the story. You know Tex Hawley was a pretty popular guy an' a pal o' yours."

*171*

That shut the constable up, and Dolan seemed to understand how the boys had felt. He drove directly to the county courthouse in Norwood, and they went inside.

There was a light in the sheriff's office. He sat slumped behind his desk. A two-day stubble of beard showed on his chin and he looked tired. But he jumped up and grinned when he saw who was entering.

"By golly, marshal," he said, "I'm glad you're here. Been trying to get you on the 'phone but they had no idea where you'd gone."

"We've been trailing Hawley and the Negro," said Dolan. "They came this way. Did they show up here?"

Sheriff Morgan shook his head. "We've had the roads guarded but no reports yet. Anyhow, they'll have trouble getting out o' this part o' the state. All the police have been alerted for a radius o' fifty miles."

"About this murder you've had on your hands," Dolan remarked. "Maybe the two cases tie together. A week ago the man Hawley was heard threatening Cherokee Sam, and he paid him money to keep him from talking. Now —if he *did* talk, and Hawley suspected it—you see?"

The sheriff looked interested. "Didn't you say you got a tip about Hawley?" he asked. "Any idea where it came from?"

"No," said Dolan. "It was last Friday—a telephone call to our office in Boston. Man wouldn't give his name but said he'd want to collect part of the reward if we caught the Kansas City bank robber. Then he told us to look for him around Quimby and hung up. We weren't able to trace the call."

There was an interruption at that moment. A perspiring deputy with a shotgun in his hand opened the door.

"We got that Comanche Injun," he announced proudly. "You want to talk to him?"

"Bring him in," said the sheriff. "What's his story?"

"Says he was asleep inside the wagon an' the sound o' the shot woke him up. Then he heard a hoss gallopin' off. When he went 'round front an' got a look at Sam he got scared. Took to the woods. We picked him up when he was tryin' to get a drink at a farmhouse well."

The handcuffed man who was pushed into the office had a dark, sullen face and long, stringy black hair. His clothes were in tatters. But even without the warpaint and the Indian regalia, Barney recognized him at once.

He repeated his account of the shooting for the sheriff, speaking fairly good English.

"Who do you think might have done it?" Dolan asked him.

"I dunno," he shrugged. "Sam kept his business to himself. We'd been doin' pretty well in the last few towns, an' I expect he had two or three hundred dollars in his poke."

"Did you find any money on this man?" Morgan asked the deputy.

"Only five dollars an' some change."

"All right. Hold him as a witness. We've got some other lines to run down."

When the Indian had been led out, the sheriff turned to Dolan's party. "You folks had any supper?" he asked. "Let's go down to the lunch wagon an' see if we can get something to eat. They'll call me there if any news breaks."

In the next half hour Barney surrounded two big hamburgers and a dish of ice cream. He tried to pay for his supper but Morgan insisted the meal was on him. They left the diner and went over to Dolan's car.

"Well," said the marshal, "I reckon I'd better take these folks back to Quimby. I'll be there tonight and tomorrow, sheriff. Call me at the Neale House if you get any news."

*　　*　　*

That was one of the longest days Chuck ever lived through. Hawley roused up after a few hours of sleep and from the middle of the morning on, he sat in the doorway or paced up and down the floor of the shack. He growled at Obadiah from time to time, cursing him for clumsiness or stupidity. Chuck lay still as a mouse, hoping to avoid the restless temper of the Texan.

Once or twice Hawley came over and tested the tightness of the ropes that bound him, but made no comment. Earlier, while the big man slept, Chuck had worked himself around with his back to the wall and dug a hole under the bottom log with his hands. The tin can was buried there, out of sight.

Late in the afternoon, Hawley and Obadiah ate the last of the bread and meat they had brought with them. They offered none of it to Chuck, and the boy began to wonder if he would ever have another meal. He felt no faintness but his stomach was cramped and hollow. Finally, when he spoke up and asked for a drink of water, the colored man brought him some.

It was about nine-thirty that night before the Texan made his preparations to leave. By candlelight he put on a dark shirt and strapped the cartridge belt with its two big guns around his waist. For a moment he hesitated about wearing the white hat, then decided to leave it on its peg. From one of the saddlebags he took a bottle of yellowish liquid which he handled with great care. Chuck wondered if it was nitroglycerin.

"I reckon that safe's pretty old," he told Obadiah. "Won't take much soup to open it. I figure to be back here by two o'clock. Have the buckboard hitched, ready to go. I'll ride the mare to the edge o' town an' go in afoot from there. Don't forget now. Keep awake, an' keep your eye on the kid. Better blow that candle out right now, 'cause somebody might see me leave here an' come snoopin' around."

Chuck waited till he heard the soft footfalls of the mare going out the trail. Then he went to work. His plan was a lot bigger than just getting his hands free. That morning he had noticed two things. One was the point of a nail jutting out of one of the poles in the wall. The other was a small lump of pine gum, dried and crystallized, that clung to a log near his head. With the help of these he meant to win his freedom.

Obadiah sat on the edge of his bunk awhile, then got up and went outdoors. Plainly he was uneasy, still worrying about the ghostly noises he thought he had heard. Occasionally the boy caught the sound of his mutterings as he paced back and forth near the stable.

The rope wasn't easy to cut through. Chuck held the can with one hand and sawed up and down with the other, keeping the hemp against the jagged edge of tin. He could sense some progress now. One after another the strands were parting. After five or ten minutes he felt the rope loosen and fall away. In the dark he started on the knots that held his ankles, and quickly untied them.

Again he picked up the empty can, centered its bottom on the projecting nail and pushed. There was a slight noise as the point came through the metal, but the colored man was still outside and gave no indication of hearing it.

Now Chuck felt around for the piece of string he had salvaged. He thought he knew where it was but for a full minute his hands searched the dirt floor in vain. Finally he got up on all fours and discovered the twine had been under him all the time. He wetted one end with his tongue, twisted it into a tight spike and tried to push it through the nail hole in the bottom of the can. It was an aggravating job, almost like threading a needle in pitch darkness.

After a dozen failures he got a shred of cotton through and picked at it till he had a firm grip on the main piece of twine. He tied a knot in it to hold it in place and reached up for the lump of rosin that had oozed out of the log. Again it took a while to find it in the dark but it broke off in his fingers just as Obadiah came back into the shack.

Chuck lay very still. If the colored man decided to light the candle and have a look at him, his whole effort was lost. But after a little more fidgety pacing, Obadiah eased himself down on the bunk. The minutes passed—valuable minutes. Chuck could picture Hawley riding the mare up to some patch of woods or brush close to the village and hiding her there, out of sight. He would probably wait till all the townsfolk had left the streets and gone to bed, but on a Monday night that wouldn't be very late. Well before midnight he should be able to reach the mill without being seen. There he would probably break a window in the office and force an entrance.

The boy waited till he was sure Obadiah was dozing, then dug out the hole under the log where he had concealed the can earlier. It took only a moment or two to work his hand clear through to the outside. Carefully he pushed the can through the opening, then pressed some dirt behind it, to hold it in place. The string, attached to the bottom, was still in his left hand. With his right he picked up the lump of pine gum and began moving it gently along the taut cord.

At first there was only a faint squeak. Then, as the fibers absorbed more of the dry rosin dust, the sound grew louder. It seemed to come from behind the cabin, somewhere in the woods outside. A long-drawn moan rose suddenly in pitch to an eerie shriek as Chuck pulled harder.

The effect on Obadiah was all he had hoped for and more. He bounded out of his bunk, shaking like a leaf. Then, as the sounds continued, he found his voice.

"Oh, Mist' Tex—Mist' Tex!" he screamed. "Whafo' you go off an' leave me? De ha'nts is after me! Dey's out dere now, a-hollerin'!"

He dove for the doorway like a scared rabbit and a moment later Chuck heard him in the stable.

"Keep me comp'ny, Jughaid!" he wailed. "Keep de ha'nts off'n me!"

The boy produced one more wild moan on the bull-fiddle, then got quietly to his feet and stole to the door.

His eyes were adjusted to the darkness and though there was no moon he could see enough to find the trail. Once, just after he left the shack, his foot snapped a twig. But the sound only served to frighten Obadiah more. As the boy hurried down the wood-road he could hear the little man alternately singing snatches of hymns and talking to the dun horse.

Chuck's only plan, now that he had escaped, was to get to a farmhouse somewhere. He remembered that there were none on the road toward Quimby, so when he reached the county highway he turned in the other direction.

The time, as near as he could guess, was somewhere around ten-thirty. At least it had been less than an hour since Hawley left the cabin.

The boy's legs had been stiff at first but they were getting limbered up now, and he moved at a steady lope. About a quarter of a mile down the road he saw a break in the woods and cleared ground beyond. And there, close to the highway, was a small house. The windows were all dark, as he had expected at this hour. Still, the place looked lived in, and he went to the front door and knocked.

At first there was silence, then he thought he heard a stirring inside. He knocked again, louder this time. An upstairs window squeaked open and a head appeared. He couldn't tell whether it was a man or a woman, but the voice, when it came, was that of a scared female.

"Who are you an' what do you want?" it quavered. "Get away from here or I'll shoot!"

"Wait, Ma'am," he said as reassuringly as possible. "All I want is some help. I'm just a boy—you can see that for yourself."

"What happened to you? What kind o' help?"

He knew his story must sound highly improbable, but he started to tell it anyhow. When he mentioned being carried on the buckboard she interrupted him.

"Hold on," she said. "That must ha' been the buckboard the man was askin' about. Robbers, eh? An' they took you along with 'em. Where are they now?"

"The really bad one's gone back to Quimby," Chuck told her. "He's getting ready to rob the mill tonight—maybe right now."

"My land o' goshen!" the old woman exclaimed. "Well, let's do somethin' about it."

She slammed the window shut and he heard her pattering down the stairs. A moment later she flung the door open, and he saw she was carrying a lantern.

"Guess I'm crazy to believe such a yarn," she said, "but I'm goin' to let you take my hoss. There's a telephone at Maitland's—that's a mile down the road towards Norwood."

She had on slippers, and a shawl was wrapped around her nightdress. At a trot she led him back to the little barn.

"Ain't time to hitch up to the buggy," she told him, "but if you can ride bareback, ol' Charlie'll take you. Good luck—an' bring him back to me when you can."

By the light of the lantern he untied the halter of the

plump gray nag and swung himself aboard. The horse
seemed a little surprised at this interruption of his slum-
bers, but he turned obediently and jogged out of the yard.
Once on the gravel road Chuck waved a grateful arm to
the old lady and dug his heels into Charlie's sides.

"Come on, boy," he urged. "We've got a job to do in
a hurry!"

**H**E RECOGNIZED the Maitland farm by the size of the buildings and the line of telephone wire that ran from a pole to the house. In the starlight, as he came closer, he could read the name on the mailbox.

He rode up the lane toward the house and dogs began barking somewhere at the back. Still holding the end of the halter he swung down and pulled the bell handle beside the front door. Again a head appeared at a screened window above, but this time it was a man who answered his summons.

"Who's there? Anything the matter?" the voice called.

"Could I use your telephone?" Chuck asked. "It's pretty important—I'm trying to stop a robbery."

The man whistled. "In that case," he said, "I'll be right down."

At the end of half a minute an electric bulb went on in the hall and the door opened. Mr. Maitland, still in his nightshirt, eyed Chuck keenly, then ushered him inside.

"Who's bein' robbed?" he asked.

"The Quimby mill. I wanted to call up Joe Paley, the constable, only I'm not sure he's got a phone."

"How 'bout the sheriff?" asked Maitland. "He's right handy here, in Norwood, an' he'd prob'ly know how to get word to the Quimby authorities."

"All right," said Chuck. "Maybe you could get him for me. I'm not much used to telephones."

The farmer chuckled and went to the forbidding looking instrument on the wall. He turned the crank, making a ringing sound, then held the receiver to his ear.

"Hi, Susan," he said after a bit. "This is Bill Maitland. Get me Sheriff Morgan, will you? No, I don't know whether he's still at the courthouse or home. Figured you'd know that. Well, try 'em both. Thanks."

The seconds dragged while Chuck waited. Then there was a squawking noise from the telephone.

"That you, sheriff?" the farmer asked. "Bill Maitland callin'. Say, there's a young feller here wants to tell you somethin'. It's about a robbery that ain't happened yet. Okay, I'll put him on."

Chuck's hand was shaking as he took the receiver, and he had to stand on tiptoe to reach the mouthpiece.

"Hello—hello," came the gruff voice at the other end of the wire. "Anybody there?"

"Yes," Chuck managed to say. "It's about Tex Hawley. He's gone back to Quimby to blow open the safe at the mill."

"What!" cried the sheriff. "Hawley? Are you sure? Say, who are you, anyway?"

"I'm Chuck Randall. I just got away from the place

they were hiding out—a choppers' shack back in the woods—"

"Hey—hold on! Are you the boy they took with 'em on the buckboard?"

"That's right. They had me tied up, but after Hawley left I managed to get loose. The colored man's still there —an' so's the box o' money."

"Well, I'll be a wall-eyed mule," the sheriff chuckled. "What a break! Listen, son, you stay right there. We'll be along in the car in two shakes of a lamb's tail. An' I'll call up the marshal in Quimby right now."

There was a click at the other end and the line went dead. Uncertainly Chuck hung up the receiver.

"He's coming in his auto," the boy told Maitland. "He wants me to stay here an' wait, but gosh! I've got to take back the old lady's horse."

The farmer laughed. "Don't worry about that. I'll see he gets back to her safe an' sound. You've got enough on your mind catchin' those robbers. Say—did they give you anything to eat?"

"Not since early this morning. Guess I'm sort o' hungry, at that."

A sudden faintness overcame him and he sat down on a chair in the hall. Maitland had disappeared, but he was back in a jiffy with a big piece of cold fried chicken, a slice of apple pie and a pitcher of milk.

"Get outside o' some o' this," he said. "You'll feel better."

Chuck took a long drink of milk and bit ravenously into the chicken. The food revived him quickly. And before he had finished, a horn tooted out in the road.

"Thanks, Mr. Maitland," he mumbled around a mouthful of pie. "Thanks an awful lot. I've got to be going."

Chuck hurried down the lane. The car waiting by the mailbox was a fairly big one and there were three men in it, two in front and one in the rear.

"Right in here with me," the sheriff called from the back seat, and Chuck climbed up beside him. The deputy who was driving put the car in gear and they chugged on in the direction of Quimby.

"I got through to Marshal Dolan all right," the sheriff told Chuck. "He'll be laying for Hawley if he shows up at the mill. Now you tell me when we get close to that hide-out o' theirs."

They passed the little house where the old lady lived. "Not much farther," Chuck said. "There's a little wood-road going off to the left. It's awful rough an' I doubt if the auto could make it."

"Suppose we leave the car here, then," Morgan suggested. "If it's pretty near we'll go in on foot."

They left the automobile at the side of the road and moved forward with Chuck in the lead. Both the deputies were armed with shotguns and the sheriff wore a revolver at his belt.

In the dark the boy almost missed the entrance to the wood-road. He was actually past it when the smell of horse came faintly to his nostrils. What little breeze there was seemed to be blowing out of the woods towards them.

He halted the posse and went back two or three steps. "Here it is," he whispered.

They proceeded as quietly as they could. The sheriff had ordered that no flashlights be used and Chuck agreed with him. But it meant they had to feel their way, moving slowly. Once one of the deputies bumped into a tree and cursed under his breath.

There was complete silence from the direction of the cabin until they were within twenty yards of the place. Then they heard the horse snort, blowing dust out of his nose. Chuck wondered if Obadiah had recovered courage enough to go back into the shack. If he had done so and found the prisoner gone, he might have decided to leave. But the fact that Jughead was still in the stable made him think the little colored man must be close by.

"All right," the sheriff whispered, "spread out an' keep me covered. I'm going to use the light."

He turned to Chuck. "Any way out o' the cabin by the back?" he asked, and the boy told him there wasn't.

The stable end of the shack was little more than a

bark-roofed shed, open its full width in front. The sheriff first turned the beam of his big three-cell torch in that direction. It shone on the rump of the dun horse but there was no sign of Obadiah.

At that moment a quavering voice called from the cabin. "Who's out dere? Dat you, Mist' Tex?"

The sheriff swung the flashlight toward the doorway. "No," he replied. "It's the law. Come out o' there with your hands up."

For answer there was a shot from the door—the blaze and the whanging report of a .44—and the bullet whistled close to Chuck's head. Instinctively he threw himself flat on the ground and the sheriff did likewise. Almost at the same instant the two deputies let go with their shotguns, but the little Negro kept on firing, apparently unhit.

"Five—six," the sheriff was counting. "All right," he yelled, "your gun's empty. Now drop it an' come out or we'll blow your head off."

He sprang to his feet and ran to the shack wall, taking cover beside the doorway. And Obadiah came stumbling out, empty-handed. His face looked twisted and gray in the beam of the flashlight, and there was blood dripping from his left arm.

"See how bad he's hurt an' bandage him up," the sheriff ordered. "Now, son, let's find the buckboard an' that box o' cash."

The buckboard had been backed into a hemlock thicket beyond the stable, where it was partially concealed. Chuck felt under the seat for the iron box, before he remembered that Hawley had taken it into the cabin. They found it stowed away beneath the bunk and hauled it out. It felt as heavy as ever.

With Morgan's help Chuck lifted it and set it outside on the ground.

"Guess we'll have to wait till we catch Hawley 'fore we try to open it," said the sheriff. "That's a pretty husky lock. Anyhow, we'll put it in the car."

He went to the shack and picked up Obadiah's abandoned six-gun. "Poor little cuss," he said. "I feel sort o' sorry for him—just got hooked up with the wrong kind o' folks, I guess."

He inspected the Negro's wound and found it wasn't serious. A few pellets from a shotgun had entered his arm, but a tight bandage had already halted most of the bleeding.

"You boys," Morgan told the deputies, "hitch up that horse to the buckboard an' take this man down to the county jail. I'm going along to Quimby an' see if we can't pick up some company for him."

He held the flashlight to his watch. "Quarter o' twelve," he said. "Maybe we'll be in time for the fireworks. Come on, son."

They carried the iron box between them down the trail to the waiting car. Then the sheriff cranked up the engine and they started.

"Anybody tell your folks what happened to you?" the older man inquired.

"Sure—bad news travels fast," said Chuck unhappily. "The trouble is they're probably still worrying. I wish there was some way to let 'em know I'm safe."

"I wouldn't wonder," said the sheriff, "if Dolan found some way to get word to 'em. That friend o' yours, Barney Burke, may have been around the hotel when I called up. Anyhow, I'll let you off at your house first."

"Oh, gosh, no!" Chuck exclaimed. "Not if you're going after Hawley. I want to be there if you'll let me."

The sheriff laughed. "I reckon you rate it," he replied. "Only if any trouble starts you'll have to keep out o' range an' try not to get hurt."

They were within half a mile of Quimby now, and Chuck watched the roadside carefully. There were fewer and fewer patches of woods, more and more houses. Then, right ahead in a little thicket of trees, he heard a low, soft whinny.

"It's the mare!" he exclaimed. "Hawley's mare. She's tied up in there. He told Obadiah he'd have to leave her an' go in on foot."

The sheriff put on the brakes and stopped close to the thicket. "Easy now," he said. "He might still be in there."

Cautiously and with revolver in hand he got out and approached the trees. Then he flashed his light through the leaves.

"Seems to be okay," he reported in a low voice. "Mighty pretty little horse. Say, sonny, can you ride?"

Chuck climbed down from the car quickly. "Yes, sir!" he said. "Where do you want me to take her?"

"Ride her home, to your house, an' tie her up there. I'll come along right behind you in the car, to pick you up."

*　　*　　*

It was more than the clouded skies that made Barney feel gloomy when he got up that Monday morning. He had lain awake a long time wondering where Hawley had taken Chuck and what he might have done to him. On the drive home the marshal had tried to reassure him.

"Maybe they thought he knew too much," Dolan said. "But more likely they figured it was safer to take him along so he couldn't tell which way they'd gone. Besides, with him on the buckboard Hawley could be pretty sure there wouldn't be any shooting if the pursuit got too close. They'll probably turn him loose, soon as they think they're safe."

When they reached Quimby, Barney had gone at once

to the Randalls'. He found them sitting at home, trying
to keep calm under the strain. Chuck's mother looked
pale, but her fingers were busy darning socks. Mr. Randall made a pretense of reading the paper, getting up
frequently to relight his pipe. Aunt Hetty was there too
—the only one who did much talking. Her eyes blazed
and she sat very straight in her chair as she spoke her
mind about the laxness of Quimby's law enforcement.

"That Joe Paley!" she sniffed. "Just a corner lounger
until he got himself appointed constable! And what did
he do? Played right into the hands of that desperado! I
knew Hawley was no good from the first time I laid
eyes on him. A cheap gambler if ever I saw one. And
now it turns out he's a bank robber, too. I'm not a bit
surprised."

"We've got a good man on the job now, though," Barney put in. "If anybody can get Chuck back safe, it's this
U. S. Marshal. He seems pretty sure Hawley'll be caught
before another day's gone. Anyhow, Chuck's too smart to
stay a prisoner very long. I bet he'll figure some way to
get away from 'em."

He said that more for Mr. and Mrs. Randall's sake than
because he really believed it. Trying to escape might be
the most foolish thing Chuck could do. After a few more
minutes the boy said good-night and went home. His

own parents weren't unduly worried, for they had had word that Barney was with the marshal.

Regardless of all that had happened that week end, the boy had his job to do. He got to the hotel a little after six and set about cleaning the stalls and watering and feeding the horses. After a while Mort Kane, the stableman, came in. He was bleary-eyed and shaky. Apparently the excitement of the race and its aftermath had been too much for him and he had gone to bed with a bottle.

"Any news?" he asked Barney.

"Not much. I was goin' to ask you the same question, but I guess you haven't seen Dolan since you got up."

"Dolan? Oh, the marshal. No, I ain't seen him since last night after the race. Is he still around?"

"Yes. He's makin' the Neale House his headquarters till this thing's settled."

By ten o'clock Barney had most of the chores done and took a few minutes off. In the dingy lobby of the hotel he found his friend Dolan sitting by the telephone reading the morning paper.

"Nothing yet," the marshal told him. "I talked to Norwood a while ago and the sheriff says Hawley hasn't left the county. With men watching every road he'd have been picked up sure if he'd tried to get out."

Late that afternoon Mort Kane came to Barney with a sheepish grin on his face. "I still feel terrible," he said.

"Wonder if you'd mind takin' the evenin' shift. I couldn't keep awake, an' my stomach's upset."

Grudgingly the boy agreed. He needed sleep himself, but the overtime would mean extra money in his weekly pay. Besides, something might break before midnight and if it did he wanted to know about it.

CHAPTER

# 16

IT WAS A LITTLE before eleven o'clock that night when the sheriff's call to Dolan came through. The marshal knew Barney was at the stable and as soon as he had hung up he hurried out to tell the boy.

"Get word to his folks that Chuck's safe," he told him. "He got away—goodness knows how—and telephoned Norwood. Don't worry about watching the stable. I've told Doane and he'll take over. Now I've got to go—your young friend says Hawley's planning to rob the mill safe. He may be there now."

Barney was off like a shot. The news gave a lift to his heart and speed to his heels. In four or five minutes he arrived, panting, at the Randalls' door. The house was dark but that made no difference. He pounded hard on the door and after a minute Mr. Randall came down in slippers and a bathrobe.

"What the—oh, it's you, Barney!" he exclaimed. "Maybe you've heard something. Quick, what is it?"

*196*

"Chuck got away from 'em," the boy told him exultantly. "I said he was too smart to stay tied up long. He got to a phone somewhere an' called the sheriff. An' he said Tex Hawley was comin' back here to rob the mill tonight!"

"The mill! I'd better get dressed fast. But thanks for the news about Chuck. I'll tell his mother."

After the door closed, Barney hurried back across the bridge. He didn't want to miss any of the excitement. Certainly nobody would have expected anything to happen after a look at Main Street. Practically everyone in the village was abed at that hour, and the place lay dark and silent. A single street light near the mill gate shone down on the empty pavement. Barney was wearing sneakers, but even so his footfalls sounded loud in his own ears. He moved over to the dark side of a big elm tree and took his stand where he had a view of the mill yard.

He had been there three or four minutes when a whisper at his elbow startled him. He looked around and saw a tall figure in dark clothes.

"Don't be scared—it's me—Dolan," said the marshal. "I've been watching here and nothing's happened so far. Doane gave me the general layout of the mill. That's the office right over there, isn't it?"

"Yes," Barney whispered. "The safe's built into the

back wall near that fourth window. You reckon he'll try to bust a pane o' glass, or would he try the door first?"

"Hard to tell. Either way we'd see him."

They lapsed into silence and stood there waiting. To the boy the minutes seemed to drag by interminably. After perhaps a quarter of an hour they heard footsteps and a man came up the street, heading for the open gate of the mill. The marshal drew his revolver but Barney recognized the newcomer.

"Wait," he whispered. "It's Mr. Randall—Chuck's dad. He's the head bookkeeper."

He ran out and intercepted the man, bringing him back to the shelter of the tree. Dolan introduced himself.

"If Hawley really plans to break in there tonight we'll have a better chance of stopping him if we wait out here. I got word to the watchman. Told him to stay away from the office so he won't get hurt," he explained. "How much cash is there in the safe?"

"A little over twelve thousand dollars," Mr. Randall replied.

"Hm—that would be worth his while," said the marshal, and again they fell silent.

*   *   *

Chuck untied the mare's bridle rein from a sapling, patted her neck to reassure her and made sure the girth was tight. Then he swung himself into the saddle. The stirrups were a bit long for him but he didn't take time to shorten them.

"Come on, girl," he said gently, and guided her out to the road.

For all her speed, Mockingbird was docile and easy to ride. Chuck trotted her along the softer ground at the side of the road and the dim kerosene headlights of the car came on behind.

The Randall house was dark when he rode into the side yard. He tethered the mare to the fence behind the wood-pile and started back toward the car. At that moment the headlamps shone on the little footbridge that crossed over the dam to the back door of the mill. And Chuck thought he saw something moving at the farther end.

"Hey!" he shouted above the chugging of the engine, and he pointed toward the bridge. But by the time he reached the sheriff's side there was nothing to be seen.

"Maybe a shadow fooled me," he told Morgan. "But it looked like a man moving toward the door."

The sheriff started the car ahead and drove nearly to the footbridge. There he turned so that the feeble beam of the lights fell directly on the narrow walkway.

"Nobody there that I can see," Morgan said. "But it's so dark at the far end I wouldn't swear to it. Anyhow, the office is 'round at the front, isn't it? I reckon that's where we'll be needed."

He backed up again and drove across the big bridge, parking a short distance from the mill and turning out the lights. With Chuck beside him he tiptoed toward the gate. They were stopped before they got there. Barney Burke appeared suddenly from the shadow of a big tree.

"Pst!" he warned, and beckoned them to follow him.

Under the tree they found the marshal and, to Chuck's surprise, his father. Mr. Randall put an arm around his shoulders.

"I heard you were all right," he whispered, "but I'm sure glad to get you home."

Barney's welcome was equally warm. "How'd you ever do it?" he asked. "Get away from 'em, I mean. You must be smarter'n I gave you credit for."

Chuck grinned in the darkness. "Just a genius, I guess," he told his chum. "An' brave an' strong, o' course. Tell you all about it some time. As a matter o' fact you gave me the idea with that bull-fiddle o' yours. What's going on—any sign o' Hawley yet?"

Barney shook his head. "Dolan an' I have been here 'most an hour. He sure hasn't been anywhere this side o' the mill."

The words "this side" clicked in Chuck's mind and he

remembered the footbridge. He was just going to say something about it when a faint glimmer of light shone for an instant through one of the office windows.

The sheriff had seen it, too, and so had Dolan. "Come on," said the marshal. "Keep quiet and follow me. There's somebody in there."

"Wait," Chuck whispered. "He must have got in the back, an' he could get out that way!"

But the others were hurrying forward, intent on reaching the office door. Chuck hesitated only an instant. Then he started running for home. He raced across the bridge and sped through the open lot. At the back door of the house he paused, listening, but there were no shots or other sounds of commotion yet. As he expected, his father had left the door unlocked. He went in quietly, not wanting to disturb his mother, but she was awake.

"That you, Evan?" she called.

Chuck ran up the stairs. "No, it's me, Mom," he said and gave her a quick kiss. "Be back soon," he told her. "They need my rifle."

In his own room he grabbed the Savage .22 and a handful of long rifle cartridges. Then, before his mother could ask more questions, he dashed downstairs and out the back door. It was only forty or fifty yards to the footbridge. He loaded the little rifle as he went across. It wasn't a very formidable weapon against a .44 Colt, but it was better than nothing.

At the farther end of the bridge he saw something that made his heart skip a beat. The mill door stood open—a blacker hole in the dark of the wall. He had been right. Hawley had entered from the back.

There was something forbidding about that gaping black door, and for a second or two the boy hesitated, screwing up his courage. Then he advanced on tiptoe and went in. The mill was so familiar to him that he needed no light to find his way.

Through the silent weave-room he moved cautiously, holding his gun ready. As he pulled open the heavy door that led to the finishing room a sound reached his ears. It was a human sound—a low groaning that came from a man in pain. Chuck was tempted to break and run, but he stood there trembling, waiting for the sound to come again. It was over to his left.

As he took a step in that direction his foot touched a metal object that rolled, and he stooped down, feeling for it in the dark. It was a big flashlight. He got his fingers around it and pressed the switch, shooting a beam of light toward the source of the groaning sound.

There on the floor lay old Jacques, the watchman. Blood was oozing from an ugly cut on his forehead. His eyes

SAWY

were closed and he appeared to be only half conscious. Chuck laid down the rifle and knelt beside him looking for other possible wounds, but his battered head was the only injury he could find.

A sudden crash of shots from the direction of the mill office brought the boy's heart into his mouth. He dropped the flashlight, still lighted, beside the watchman and picked up his rifle. Then, as the door to the shipping room flew open, he ducked behind one of the inspection tables, pulling back the bolt that cocked the gun.

In the dim light thrown by the torch on the floor he saw a burly figure backing through the door, blazing away with a six-gun. A handkerchief covered the lower part of the face, but Chuck knew it was Hawley.

The Texan turned, tripped over a roll of cloth and swore as he picked himself up. Chuck's hands steadied on the rifle. He didn't want to shoot, yet he knew he had to or the bandit would get away. He aimed at the hurrying target and pulled the trigger.

Above the sharp crack of the rifle he heard Hawley swear again but he kept on at a stumbling run, making for the weave-room door. And there, as he reached for the handle, he slumped heavily to his knees.

Before Chuck could make up his mind about leaving the shelter of the table, the electric lights went on overhead. Through the door from the shipping room came Dolan, gun in hand, and close behind him were the sheriff, Barney and Chuck's father. The Texan had dropped his six-shooter. Now he tried unsteadily to hold up his hands.

"Don't shoot," he groaned. "I give up."

The marshal moved in to take his prisoner and Chuck chose that moment to step out from behind the table. Instantly Sheriff Morgan whirled, covering him with his gun. Then he grinned and lowered the weapon.

"So that was you, young feller," he said. "I heard the shot an' thought it sounded like a small-caliber rifle. Seems to have done the trick, though. Who's that, lying over yonder?"

"The watchman," Chuck told him. "Old Jacques. He must have heard Hawley break in the back door an' come in here to see what was up. He got hit on the head an' he's bleeding pretty bad."

The sheriff and Mr. Randall picked the old Frenchman up between them and carried him back to the mill office where they laid him on a settee. Chuck's father called up Dr. Timmins and routed him out of bed.

"Got a patient for you down here at the mill," he told him. "It's the watchman—got hit on the head trying to stop a robbery."

"Two patients," Dolan put in from the doorway. "Our

Mr. Hawley's got a .22 slug between his ribs. Don't think he'll die of it, though. He's more likely to hang."

*   *   *

The rest of the week was quiet enough after that exciting night. Chuck's father thought the boy had earned a holiday and he didn't go back to work until Wednesday. Tuesday he spent catching up on his sleep and gabbing with Barney, at the hotel stable.

"You sure timed it right last night," the Irish boy told him. "It took us longer'n we expected, because we had to make sure the light in the office wasn't just old Jacques lookin' around. We waited at the windows until Hawley struck another match, an' we could see him on his knees in front o' the safe. He had his tools laid out, ready to go to work. Your dad had the key to the front door, an' as soon as he put it in the lock Tex heard the noise an' jumped up. He left his tools an' backed out, shooting at us on the way. One bullet put a hole in the top o' Dolan's hat!"

The little Mockingbird mare was quartered at the hotel temporarily, and between them the boys gave her so much grooming and petting she was in a fair way to be spoiled.

When he started work again, Chuck found himself the center of interest among the weavers and finishers. Even

206

from the dye house and the carding room people came around to look at him and ask him questions. At first the role of hero was flattering but he soon got tired of the attention. It was a relief when things settled back to normal, though he did have one pleasant surprise. When he was paid on Saturday he got a full week's wages, in spite of having been out two days.

He went swimming with Barney that Sunday afternoon. As they lay on the bank afterward, reveling in the hot, clear sunshine, Chuck was brought up to date on the Hawley case.

"Dolan's gone back to Boston," Barney told him. "He was sure glad to clean up the case, for the government's been tryin' to find the guy that robbed that bank ever since March. He says there was 'most twenty thousand dollars in the iron box! That's more'n half o' what was stolen. Hawley probably won't ever have to stand trial for the robbery, though. He broke down when he thought he was goin' to die from your bullet. Told the sheriff he'd killed Cherokee Sam to keep him from talkin'. So the county gets first crack at him on a murder charge."

"What about Obadiah?" Chuck asked. "I don't believe he had anything to do with it."

"He'll most likely get off with a light sentence. Ninety days at the County Farm is about all they think he'll be given."

"Good," said Chuck. "I sort of liked the little guy, even when I was scaring the daylights out of him. Gosh, you'd have laughed your head off, the way he hollered when I started to rub the string on that bull-fiddle!"

After they were dressed Barney asked a casual question—almost too casual, Chuck thought afterwards.

"You goin' to be at work tomorrow?" he inquired.

"O' course. What do you mean, am I going to be at work?"

"Nothin'," Barney smiled. "Just wondered, that's all."

CHAPTER

# 17

CHUCK WAS STILL CURIOUS about his friend's remark as
he crossed the footbridge Monday morning. Then he
pitched into the daily round of tasks and forgot it for the
next few hours.

But at ten o'clock he was reminded of the question once
more. MacPherson, the finishing room foreman, came
over to him, a queer look on his seamed Scotch face. "Ye're
wanted in the front office," he said, rolling his r's even
more than usual.

Chuck was a little dazed. "What's the matter?" he
asked. "What do they want me for? Or maybe it's just
Dad wants to tell me something."

"Stop your questions an' go," the foreman advised.
"An' brush the lint off your shirt on the way."

The boy made his way through the shipping room and
opened the office door. What he saw inside startled him.
There was his mother, in her best Sunday dress—and

209

Barney Burke—and Sheriff Morgan. Beyond them stood Amos Sawyer, owner of the mill, and his son Clinton. Of course Chuck's father was on hand, as well as Aunt Hetty and the rest of the office staff.

Chuck stood there in his work clothes, not knowing what to do or to say. The whole group was looking at him, some smiling, some solemn.

Amos Sawyer cleared his throat nervously. With all his wealth and business acumen he was a shy man, diffident about speaking in public.

"Er—ah—Miss Hetty," he said, "would you explain to the young man—er—why we've asked him here?"

The spry little lady smiled and stepped forward. "Chuck," she addressed her nephew, "Mr. Sawyer feels sort of grateful to you. Like all the rest of us he's proud that a Quimby boy had the spunk to outwit that—that desperado—and save the company's money. So here in this box is a gift he wants you to have, a token of his appreciation."

From behind her she brought out a little red leather box and placed it in Chuck's grimy hand. Gingerly he opened the lid and there, gleaming against the velvet lining, was a beautiful gold watch.

"Gosh!" he breathed. "I—I don't know what to say."

"You don't have to say a word," Aunt Hetty beamed. "Sheriff Morgan's going to do the talking now."

The gray-haired sheriff chuckled. "It's a pleasure—what I've got to tell you, son," he said. "Seems the bank, out in Kansas City, posted a reward after that robbery. The U. S. Marshal's office agreed with me that if anybody was responsible for catchin' the bank robber it was a young feller by the name o' Charles Henry Randall."

He paused and took a piece of paper out of his pocket. "That's the name on this check," he continued, "an' it's for a thousand dollars. Looks to me like you'll have a nice nest-egg to start college, when you're ready."

Still speechless, Chuck stared at the check in his hand. A thousand dollars! As much money as he could make if he worked two years in the mill! His head was in a whirl.

But the sheriff wasn't through yet, it appeared. He pushed Barney forward.

"Both o' you boys had a part in bringin' Hickson, alias Hawley, to justice. I figure Barney, here, deserves some sort of a reward, too. It's the county's job to dispose o' property that's confiscated from criminals. An' among the things Hawley won't be needin' any more is that little racin' mare o' his. I understand Barney's partial to horses an' as long as he's already taken a shine to this one, we're goin' to turn Mockin'bird over to him for keeps."

Barney had been grinning like an imp, enjoying every moment of his friend's embarrassment. Now suddenly it was his turn to be tongue-tied. His jaw fell open and his eyes almost popped out of their sockets.

"Y-you mean," he stammered, "the mare's goin' to be m-mine?"

Sheriff Morgan nodded emphatically. "Think you can keep her in feed?" he asked with a twinkle.

"Oh, boy—can he!" cried Chuck. He held his gifts in one hand and flung the other arm around Barney's neck. In his delight at his friend's good fortune he forgot all about his loss of words.

The party broke up in a general round of hand-shaking by the men and hugs by Mrs. Randall and Aunt Hetty. Clint Sawyer, who seemed subdued and a little crestfallen, pulled Barney aside.

"Just for fun, some time," he said, "I'd like to run that race over. No bets—except maybe a chocolate soda. I still think Planter's Punch can beat the mare."

"Sure," the Irish boy replied. "I'll start gettin' her ready. Just remember, though—she won't be luggin' any two hundred pounder this time!"

*　　*　　*

That evening the boys sat out under the tree back of the Randalls' house and talked.

"What a summer!" said Barney with a contented sigh. "I guess there'll never be another one like it."

"You're right," Chuck answered. "Who'd have thought, that night last spring when we were spearing suckers an' saw the stranger on the buckboard, it would ever end up like this?"

Barney rose and stretched. "I better be gettin' home an' see if Mockin'bird's comfortable," he remarked. "What time do you reckon it is?"

Soberly Chuck pulled the gold watch out of his pocket.

"It's exactly twenty-four and a half minutes past eight," he announced.